PYRATES #4

THE LAST CLUE

CHRIS ARCHER

SCHOLASTIC INC.

New York Toronto London Auckland Sydney
Mexico City New Delhi Hong Kong Buenos Aires

No part of this publication may be reproduced in whole or in part, or stored in a retrieval system, or transmitted in any form or by any means, electronic, mechanical, photocopying, recording, or otherwise, without written permission of the publisher. For information regarding permission, write to Scholastic Inc., Attention: Permissions Department, 557 Broadway, New York, NY 10012.

ISBN 0-439-36854-5

Copyright © 2003 17th Street Productions,
an Alloy, Inc. company
All rights reserved.
Published by Scholastic Inc.

Produced by 17th Street Productions,
an Alloy, Inc. company
151 West 26th Street
New York, NY 10001

SCHOLASTIC and associated logos are trademarks and/or
registered trademarks of Scholastic Inc.

12 11 10 9 8 7 6 5 4 3 2   3 4 5 6 7 8/0

Printed in the U.S.A.   40
First printing, April 2003

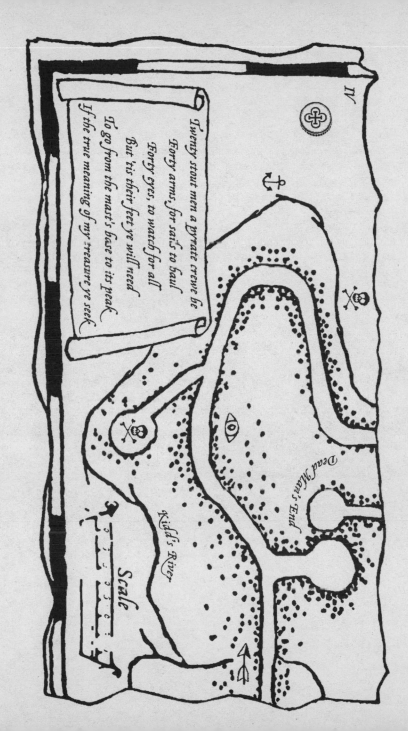

Twenty stout men a pyrate crewe be
Forty arms, for sails to haul
Forty eyes, to watch for all
But 'tis their feet ye will need
To go from the mast's base to its peak
If the true meaning of my treasure ye seek

Dead Man's End

Kidd's River

Scale

IV

One

KIDNAPPED!

George van Gelder stood in his dusty living room, his heart thumping in his chest. Across from him sat his dad, who was normally calm and collected but now seemed stunned, scared, and frustrated. He held his head in one hand and a folded piece of writing paper in the other. On the table in front of him was an antique letter seal that was strung on a simple silver chain. George recognized the seal. It belonged to his dad's colleague, Professor Kira Trenov.

George felt terrible, because he knew he was responsible—for all of it.

"Dad," he said slowly, his voice trembling a little as he spoke, "I have something to tell you."

George's dad looked up at him curiously. He shifted his hands to his lap, and George could see the angry dark writing of the note that had upset his father. *Dr. van Gelder,* it read,

I have Professor Kira Trenov. The seal is proof that I have her. I am not afraid to hurt

her. And I will do just that if you do not bring the diamond to me. You know what I mean. I know that you have it or that you will have it soon. If you haven't found it yet, you'd better hurry. You only have until noon tomorrow. At that time I will call and give you instructions on how to bring it to me.

Don't contact the police. I'll know.

—Leroy

"You have something to tell me?" his dad asked with furrowed brows. He looked like he wasn't sure whether to be hopeful or angry. "What is it, George? Do you know something about this?"

George gulped, his heart jumping into his throat. The truth was, George knew *everything* about it. He had been lying to his dad for weeks. And now things had gone too far. His father's friend Kira was being held by a dangerous criminal. George had never thought it would come to this.

It was time to come clean.

"I—I do know about it, Dad." Peter van Gelder looked up in surprise, and George's heart sank. How could he tell him? "I'm so sorry. I think this is all *my* fault."

"*Your* fault?" His dad frowned at him, clearly baffled. "George, what are you talking about?"

George took a deep breath. *Well, here goes nothing.* "First of all, Dad, you're not going to believe this . . . but Leroy? The Leroy who signed the note?"

George's dad nodded rapidly. "Yes? I have no idea who this Leroy is. I don't know anyone named Leroy."

"Well . . . this is going to sound a little crazy, Dad." George paused. The truth was, he didn't know whether his father would believe him. "But Leroy is just a code name for Mr. Roulain."

George's dad's eyebrows shot up. He didn't seem to know what to make of this. "Mr. Roulain? Our neighbor Mr. Roulain? I find that very hard to believe, George. He's been our friend for years. Why would he need a code name? And more to the point, what could he possibly want with Kira?" Mr. van Gelder looked utterly confused.

Oh, man, George thought. *If he has a hard time believing that, how am I going to tell him about everything else?*

"I know it sounds crazy, Dad. But I swear it's true! Roulain is bad news. Derrick, Renee, and Shannon will back me up on this. They're all involved. In fact, maybe they should come over so we can all go through it together. It's kind of complicated."

George's dad sighed, looking from George to the note and back again. "All right, George. I don't understand why your friends need to be here, but have them come quickly. We don't have much time." His dad winced as he looked at his watch. "I can't believe someone's kidnapped Kira," he murmured. "I'll go in the kitchen and make some tea. You call your friends."

George nodded quickly and ran for the phone. He dialed his best friend, Derrick, first. As he explained Kira's kidnapping, his brain was working overtime trying to sort out everything that had happened so far. Kira Trenov was a new friend of his father's. She came from Litaria, one of the countries his father studied as a professor of eastern European history. Litaria was also the original home of a priceless diamond that had occupied George's every thought for the last few weeks. The gem was called the Eye of Eternity, and George and his friends had been convinced just an hour ago that they had all the clues they needed to find it.

"Kira?" Derrick asked after George had repeated the whole story. *"Leroy* has her? What do you think he wants with her?"

"He thinks we have the diamond," George explained simply. "Or if we don't have it, he thinks we can get it. He must've given up on finding the Eye of Eternity himself. Now he wants us to do it for him."

"Whoa," Derrick said under his breath. George

could hear the disbelief in Derrick's voice. While they all knew they were putting themselves at risk going up against Leroy, none of them had thought their treasure hunt would endanger anyone else. "Does your dad know what's going on yet?"

George glanced over at his father, who was watching him from the kitchen table. *Hurry*, his father mouthed at him. He pointed to his watch frantically. George nodded and answered Derrick.

"No," he said. "We need to explain it all. Fast."

"Gotcha," Derrick replied. "Well, I'll call Shannon and tell my parents where I'm going, and then I'm on my way. See you in a few."

"See you." George hung up the phone. Then he called Renee and had the same conversation. "They're coming," he said to his father after Renee promised to rush over. "I'll be right back, Dad. I need to get something."

George ran up the steep stairway that led to the second floor, where his bedroom was. He got down on his hands and knees and tugged a cardboard box out from under his bed. Carefully he took off the lid and pulled out three pieces of paper. He remembered the first time he had seen each of the ancient papers. It seemed like a really long time ago. *I never thought it would depress me to look at this stuff,* he thought. *But I guess I never thought it would get this serious.* He ran a hand over the papers' rough surface and sighed. Then he grabbed a small wooden chest from the bottom of his closet and brought everything downstairs.

Just as he placed all of the items on the kitchen table, the doorbell rang. George jumped. "I'll get that, Dad." Peter van Gelder nodded and began to look through the papers as George ran to the front door. He opened it to greet Shannon and Renee on the front steps, both gasping to catch their breath. Shannon's red-and-orange-streaked dark hair was whisked back in a bandanna. Renee wore her long blond hair in a ponytail, but a few pieces had fallen out. George glanced at his watch. "Wow, guys. That's gotta be a record."

"We . . . came . . . as . . . fast as we . . . could," Shannon panted, leaning against the wall for support. "I told . . . my mom . . . you needed help . . . with the math homework. I can't . . . believe it about Kira. Does your dad know everything?"

George shook his head. Renee sighed and glanced down the street. "Here comes Derrick."

George could see his best friend rounding the corner and plowing toward his front steps, running faster than George had ever seen him go.

"Hey . . . George," Derrick greeted the group breathlessly. "Shannon . . . Renee." He looked up at George. "So . . . is your dad inside?"

George nodded. "Come on in, guys. I haven't told him anything yet, except that we know Leroy is Roulain. We've got some explaining to do."

Shannon groaned as the three of them followed him into the house. "I can't believe this is happening."

George led the way back into the kitchen, where his father had already spread out the three pieces of paper on the table. He was looking from one to the other, frowning at them thoughtfully.

"Hi, Mr. van Gelder," Shannon greeted him.

"Hello, everyone." Peter van Gelder nodded at each of George's friends, then rubbed his hand against his chin. "George, if I'm not mistaken, you've got three out of four pieces of a rudimentary treasure map here. The original piece appears to be at least three hundred years old. Where did you get this?"

George looked at his dad in surprise. *He's pretty quick,* George thought. "Um, you're right, Dad. It *is* a treasure map. We have three pieces, and if I'm right, we have what we need to get the fourth. Let me just try something."

He picked up the antique seal that Leroy had sent his dad with the note. The seal was originally from Litaria, and it had once belonged to Kira Trenov's ancestor. At lunch that day George's friends had helped him figure out why the shape looked so familiar—it was a key.

"George!" Peter van Gelder exclaimed. "What are you doing? That's an heirloom. It's very valuable to Kira."

"I know, Dad, but it'll be more valuable if it helps save her life," George replied. "Just trust me."

George's dad nodded with a sigh and watched as his son gently placed the seal in the lock of the small wooden chest. George could feel his friends holding their breath as he applied just a little pressure, then a little more. The seal turned in the lock just as easily as a brand-new key.

Shannon gasped. "That's it," she said softly.

The lock sprang open with a tiny *snick,* and George pulled the lid of the chest open.

"Whoa," Derrick murmured as George reached in and gently pulled out an ancient, yellowing piece of paper. "You know what this means?"

George nodded as he arranged the paper next to the other three pieces, creating one big map of a circular system of tunnels. "Yeah," he said, tracing the tunnels with his finger. "It means we have the last clue."

Two

The Truth

"It all started," George began explaining, "on my birthday. After my party, when you were returning the costumes, we kind of . . ." He looked around at his three friends. Shannon and Derrick looked a little ashamed. "Well, Derrick and Shannon and I kind of sneaked into the attic."

Peter van Gelder looked more confused than angry. The five of them were sitting around the kitchen table, George and his friends trying to explain what they knew to his father. "Okay," George's dad said slowly. "And then . . ."

"We found a map up there, Dad," George said. He pointed to the top-left map. "It was this one. Well, it looked like this. I accidentally locked the real one back in the secret compartment of your desk, but Derrick has a photographic memory and re-created it." George looked up at his father. "The originals were drawn by Captain Kidd."

George watched as his father's eyes widened. Peter van Gelder cocked his head to the side and examined the maps, a little frown on his face. George knew that his dad had to realize what George was saying wasn't all that far-fetched. They lived in a single-family house that had been built in the late 1600s and passed down through George's mother's family for generations. The original owners had been Sarah Oort, George's great-times-eight grandmother, and her first husband, who was the infamous pirate known as Captain Kidd.

George's dad nodded slowly. "Ohhh-kay. Go on."

So George did. He explained all about where the maps led—to the tunnels that extended all over the southern tip of Manhattan. And he explained how they had accessed them from George's basement. About the journal they'd found—Captain Kidd's *real* journal—that had given them clues to find a second map, which had given them clues to find a third, and so on. And about Paul, the orphan boy they'd met in the tunnels who had helped navigate the confusing underground world.

It was an unbelievable story, George knew. He never would've believed it himself if it hadn't happened to him. George watched his dad's face grow more and more confused as the story went on. By the time George was finished, he might as well have been telling his dad that he fought with the Knights of the Round Table and kept a pet dragon in the basement.

"George, I can't believe you. You're telling me we have a *secret door* downstairs that leads to a system of secret tunnels under the city?" his dad asked, shaking his head in disbelief. "We have a serious problem on our hands. This is not the time to make up stories!"

Shannon jumped up and put a reassuring hand on Peter van Gelder's shoulder. "I know it sounds crazy, Mr. van Gelder," she said earnestly, "but it *is* true. Every word of it. We can *prove* it to you!"

Shannon took a few steps toward the basement and turned back toward her friends. "Come on, guys, let's show George's dad the trapdoor."

"Oh, yeah!" Derrick chimed in. "Once you see the tunnels, Mr. van Gelder, you'll know that there's no way we made this up."

Peter van Gelder rose uncertainly to his feet, then followed a few steps behind George and his friends. "All right, kids," he said. "I'll take a look, but I hope it's somehow related to Kira. Otherwise we're wasting precious time. I don't know what else to do but call the police."

"That's a bad idea, Dad," George said as Shannon opened the basement door and they all trooped down the steep, narrow stairs in the dim light of the basement's single bulb. He was remembering one of the last times they'd been in the tunnels . . . he had overheard some of Roulain's henchmen talking about how Leroy had an "in" with the police. "I think Roulain has some friends in high places. I believe him when he says he would know if we called the cops. We've got to be careful."

Peter van Gelder heaved a huge sigh. By now they were down in the basement, approaching the tiny room beneath the house's fireplace where a trapdoor opened down to a long, dark tunnel. "I'm trying to think of what's safest, George," he said sadly. "For us and for Kira. We might not have another choice."

The door that led to the underground tunnels was hidden by dozens of huge boxes of books that had to be moved every time they wanted to go underground. Shannon started pushing aside the boxes, and George, Renee, and Derrick quickly joined her as George's dad looked on with a skeptical expression. When they were done, George grabbed a flashlight from the spot where the group stashed their gear, in a corner that was usually hidden by boxes, and pointed it into the tiny room.

"Look, Dad," he said simply.

George's dad stared in surprise at the trapdoor in the floor. George could imagine what his father was thinking. He'd lived in this house since before George was even born, and he'd never noticed this tiny room in the basement before. George hadn't known about it, either, until just a few weeks ago. He and his friends believed that it had once been part of the house's chimney. Peter van Gelder glanced at George suspiciously, and George simply nodded toward the small room, prompting his father to check it out.

"Go on, Mr. van Gelder," Derrick urged. "Take a look."

George watched as his father hesitantly folded up his tall, thin frame and angled himself into the small room, looking around curiously. He looked all around each of the walls, then straight up at the ceiling that was also their fireplace's floor. Then, finally, he looked down at the ground where the trapdoor lay. He knelt down, brushing his hand over the ancient wooden door.

"I don't believe this," he said softly, looking at George in a kind of sheepish surprise. "Your mother would have loved this, you know? Secret rooms and hidden trapdoors. She would have had to investigate if she had known this was here."

George nodded. His mother had been fascinated by pirates, just like he had. George had wished more than once that she could have been a part of their treasure hunt. She had loved adventure. George knew his dad was different—he was into history, but he really liked facts. He was sensible, careful, and logical. But he was about to get a big surprise.

George watched as his father grasped the octagonal handle, pulled the door open, and peered inside. George moved closer and aimed the flashlight down into the hole, but the beam found only darkness. There was a long, narrow drop from this door into the first tunnel. Peter van Gelder's eyes widened in surprise.

"We use ropes and harnesses to lower ourselves down there," George told his father. "At the bottom is a tunnel. It connects to other tunnels that lead all over lower Manhattan."

George's dad reached a hand into the hole, shaking his head. "I wonder how deep it is," he said in a faraway voice.

"Maybe forty or fifty feet." George tried to read his father's expression. But Peter van Gelder just backed away from the hole and shook his head.

"Well," he said, looking stunned, "okay, then." He didn't seem to know what else to say. *He can't believe it,* George thought. *He can't picture me dropping down into that hole or following the maps.* "I guess . . . I don't know if I should apologize for not believing you or yell at you for doing all this behind my back."

George tried to smile. He knew that his father was struggling with a lot of new information. "That's okay, Dad. I wouldn't have believed it myself."

George's dad nodded. "I guess what's most important is how this connects Kira to Mr. Roulain," he said. "And what about the diamond?"

George took a deep breath. Where to begin?

"Let's go back upstairs," Renee said, "and we'll tell you all the rest of it. And then we can try to decide what to do."

George and his friends trooped back up the stairs with his father behind them. *We'd better hurry,* he thought as they walked into the kitchen and sat down around the maps again. *We don't have the diamond—and we don't have much time to find it.*

As quickly as he could, George told his father about the danger—more than he wanted to admit—that they'd faced in trying to get all four maps. Rocks had tumbled from the booby-trapped tunnel ceilings, almost crushing them! George had fallen into a pool of quicksand and almost drowned! And finally—*most* terrifying—Mr. Roulain, George's favorite neighbor, had kidnapped George and Shannon when he'd realized that they were following Captain Kidd's maps. This was how they'd discovered that mild-mannered Mr. Roulain was actually the greedy, ruthless Leroy—the master of the underworld.

George went on to tell his dad about how he and

his friends had read in Captain Kidd's journal that the treasure was actually the Eye of Eternity—a famous diamond that rightfully belonged to the monarchy of Litaria. The kids had grilled George's dad when they'd discovered the connection between the treasure and the little country in eastern Europe. They'd learned that the diamond—stolen from the Litarian king more than three hundred years ago—held a special, almost magical meaning for the people of Litaria. The Litarian people believed that the diamond gave their leaders wisdom and power.

"I wondered why you had suddenly taken such an interest in my work," his father said with a vague smile. "All this time it wasn't for a history report, but a treasure hunt."

"Roulain is after the diamond, too," George explained, "and he's also dealing with a lot of other illegal stuff. He's got all kinds of things stashed down in the tunnels—DVD players and stereos and paintings, things that we think must be stolen. He has all these thugs working for him, and he's scared away all the homeless people who used to live down in the tunnels." George could sense his father's bewilderment as he looked into his worried eyes. He almost wished he'd never even heard of Captain Kidd.

"Well." George's dad took a deep breath and

seemed to be trying to absorb everything. "George, I wish you had told me about this earlier. From what you've told me, you could have been hurt, and now Kira . . ." He shook his head as if he couldn't think about it.

"I know, Dad," George said. "I just wanted to find the treasure so much. It was so amazing to be following the path Captain Kidd laid out for us. I knew if I told you, you'd tell me to stop looking for it."

Peter van Gelder's expression softened. "You're right." He sighed. "I would have stopped you to try to keep you safe. But now we don't have much choice. We have to figure out how to proceed. How to save Kira."

George and his friends nodded solemnly. What George hadn't mentioned was that all this time, he'd been more than a little suspicious of Kira. She'd shown up exactly at the same moment they began their search for the diamond, and she'd been spending a *lot* of time at the van Gelders' house.

Was it coincidence that the search for the diamond had turned scary just as Kira arrived on the scene?

Could this woman have been hanging around just to listen to George's father talk about the country of Litaria? She was *from* Litaria. Why did she need to listen to a history professor talk about her own country? It was possible, George thought, that she had made up the story about her connection to the Litarian people just to get close to George and his father.

Kira might be looking for the diamond for her own reasons. In fact, she could even be *working* with Roulain on this whole thing.

"George, what about the mystery woman who you said you saw down in the tunnels a couple of times?" Renee asked suddenly out of nowhere. "Is there any way that could have been Kira?"

George turned to Renee in amazement. Was she reading his mind?

"Yeah," Shannon said, "if that was Kira and she was slinking around down in the tunnels, it kind of suggests that she's involved with Roulain in some way. Maybe she wasn't kidnapped at all. Maybe she helped set this trap. Plus it was her seal that opened the chest. That's a pretty big coincidence."

"Well, remember," Derrick spoke up, "that tombstone where we dug up the chest said 'Sergei Trenov.' Sergei Trenov could have been an ancestor of Kira's, right? Has she ever mentioned him to you, Mr. van Gelder?"

Peter van Gelder looked from Derrick to George. He looked a little lost. "Sergei Trenov?" he said after a moment. "Yes, actually, she *has*. The seal she wore around her neck belonged to a Sergei

Trenov. She had a whole story to go with it. . . .
Sergei Trenov was leaving on an expedition, and he
left the seal with his wife. Legend has it that the
purpose of this expedition was to—"

"To meet with *Captain Kidd*," George finished.
"He was supposed to be meeting with Captain
Kidd to take the Eye of Eternity back to Litaria.
But he never returned from his expedition. And
down in the tunnels there was a tombstone—"

"*A tombstone?*" George's dad frowned. "Oh, that
doesn't sound good."

"It was where we found the third map," George
continued. "The tombstone said—"

"*Here lyes Sergei Trenov,*" Derrick supplied.
"*Wrongly accused. Unjustly killed. 1701.*"

For a moment George, his friends, and his father
all looked at each other silently, nobody wanting to
be the first to speak. George knew that everyone in
the room was feeling sorry for him—sorry that he
idolized a bloodthirsty, booby-trapping pirate. They
believed that Captain Kidd had lured Sergei Trenov
into a trap and killed him . . . just like the cruel,
vengeful pirate that everyone believed he was. That
was what Kira Trenov believed, too—that Captain
Kidd was a killer who had murdered her ancestor.
But George didn't believe that. In Kidd's journal he
had read about Sergei Trenov's plan to retrieve the

diamond—and about how Captain Kidd was afraid of being tricked by the Litarian government. There had to be an explanation for what had happened to Sergei Trenov. Why would Captain Kidd kill a man to prevent him from getting the diamond, only to bury it in a tunnel underneath his house? Why would Kidd himself engrave the words *unjustly killed* on Sergei's tombstone—if *he* had killed him? And besides . . .

"Captain Kidd was hanged in 1701. He would have been in England already, for his trial. So how could he have killed Sergei Trenov?" George asked.

Nobody made any response. But George could see the wheels turning in his friends' minds. He knew he had a point.

There had to be an explanation.

"Anyway," Derrick said finally, "she could have been down there researching this guy's death. That's all I'm saying."

"I don't think so, Derrick," Peter van Gelder said slowly. "I don't believe she actually knew that Sergei Trenov was killed here. I can't imagine how she would have found out about these tunnels running under our house. *I* certainly never would have imagined them if I hadn't seen them." He paused. "Tell me more about this mystery woman, George."

George explained to him that twice he thought

he'd seen a woman skulking around down in the tunnels. She was dressed all in black, and they had never seen her up close. Given her shape and size, he believed it could have been Kira Trenov. Then again, it could easily have *not* been her. Once he had thought it looked like Mrs. St. John from next door.

George's dad frowned. "Tell me something, kids. Can you tell me when you saw this woman? Maybe I was *with* Kira one of those times. That would prove that it couldn't have been her."

"Okay, yeah, good idea, Dad." George frowned, trying to remember. "Let's see. I think one time was when you were out at the St. Johns' playing bridge. Remember? We'd just talked about Litaria. It was at night, and you had your weekly game."

George's dad frowned in concern. "You went down there at *night*?"

George wasn't sure what to say.

Then George's dad shook his head. "Never mind. That was silly of me." He furrowed his brows and tried to think. "Actually, I do remember. The truth is, George, I wasn't at the St. Johns'. Mrs. St. John couldn't play that night because she had to meet with her lawyers, so I went out with Kira. It was the first time we actually planned to go out—you know, like a date." He looked a little sheepish. In fact, George thought he might be blushing a little.

"But why didn't you tell me you were out with her? You said you were playing bridge." Something about all this bugged him. Why couldn't his dad have told him the truth?

"I don't know, George. I guess I just didn't know how you'd feel about it. But it's good news that it wasn't Kira, right? She can't be the mystery woman."

George considered his dad's words. "Okay, I guess it wasn't Kira." This whole business about his father wanting to spend time with Kira struck him as odd. He seemed to really *like* her, and George wasn't sure what to make of it. "Well, the other person I thought it might have been was Mrs. St. John," George said. "I mean, I know it seems crazy, but it really looked a lot like her, from what I could see."

"Oh, for Pete's sake, George." George's dad laughed. "Is there anyone we know who you *don't* think is involved in this?"

"I guess you're right," George said slowly. "I kind of figured it couldn't have been her."

"Hey, wait a minute," Derrick broke in. "The idea is to cover all our bases. I mean, we should really follow all our leads, no matter how crazy, right?" He turned to Mr. van Gelder. "If someone had told you a week ago that you'd be looking for pirate treasure under your house and your new girlfriend would be kidnapped by your next-door neighbor, wouldn't you have thought it was just crazy talk?"

George's dad made a face. "Well, I wouldn't say 'girlfriend,' exactly, Derrick. I mean, it's only been a couple of dates."

"Come *on,* Mr. van Gelder, that's not what I'm talking about."

George's dad looked kind of embarrassed. "Yes, okay, you're probably right," he said, nodding. "I suppose it wouldn't hurt to *ask* Mrs. St. John. Although she's going to think it sounds preposterous."

George looked over at Derrick, Shannon, and Renee, thinking about how weird it felt for him and his friends to be in charge here, while his dad sort of followed their lead. It felt good but also kind of scary. In a way, he wanted his dad to have all the answers.

It was Renee who finally broke the silence. "Well, are we going to go over to the St. Johns' or what?"

"Yeah, let's go," George said, standing up.

Shannon's eyes widened as they neared the front door. "You don't think Roulain's *watching* us, do you?"

Peter van Gelder looked out the window and frowned. "I don't think so, but even if he is, it won't do him much good to mess with us. He *needs* us to find that diamond."

"Besides," Derrick added as they walked to the front door, "why would he care if we talked to the St. Johns?"

Three

ROULAIN'S VICTIM

Shannon nodded, and Derrick pulled open the door. They all walked across the short stretch of sidewalk to the St. Johns' door. The St. Johns had been the van Gelders' neighbors for George's whole life. He'd been to their house lots of times. They were almost like family—they often dropped by just to say hello. Plus, George's dad played bridge with them every Tuesday night—*unless he's on a date with Kira,* George thought.

Still, this visit was different. George kept an eye out as his dad knocked on the door. There wasn't anyone else on the street, but that didn't mean they weren't being watched.

"Well, well, well!" Mrs. St. John greeted the troop on her front steps. "What a surprise to find all of you on my doorstep. And looking a little the worse for wear, I should say." She smiled warmly. "Welcome! Would you like to come in and sit down? I could make a pot of tea. . . ."

"That's okay, Mrs. St. John. We don't really

have time for tea. We just want to talk for a minute," George said.

"Eleanor," Peter van Gelder began, "there is something we need to talk to you about. It's rather pressing. But I should warn you: It will sound a little strange."

"Well, I suppose," Mrs. St. John said, seeming concerned now. She backed away from the door and led them all into the living room.

"It seems that to my great surprise," Mr. van Gelder began, looking uncomfortable, "there are some . . . well . . . underground tunnels running under the neighborhood. I mean, a system of navigable tunnels. Accessible from my basement and, I gather, a number of other places."

Mrs. St. John just nodded, as if they were talking about the most normal thing in the world. "Please continue," she urged.

"Well, the kids have been down there, um, exploring."

"I see," Mrs. St. John said, a slight crease appearing between her eyebrows.

George could see that his dad was having some trouble getting the story out, so he decided to break in. "Mrs. St. John, the thing is, when we were down in the tunnels, we kept seeing a woman dressed in black, following us. It was really far away, but I thought she looked a lot like you. I mean, it was dark and everything, but we were wondering if it was you, and if you might have any information about what's going on down there."

George's dad jumped in. "I know it sounds bizarre, Eleanor, and we certainly don't mean to imply—"

Mrs. St. John looked from George to his father. "No, it *was* me," she said.

"It—it *was*?" Mr. van Gelder blurted out.

George's mouth dropped open in shock. Sure, he'd thought the woman in the tunnels had *sort of* resembled Mrs. St. John—but why would she be down there?

"It certainly was, Peter. And I can't believe that you kids were actually *playing* down there! It's so dangerous! I didn't see you, George, but if I had, my very *first* order of business would have been to tell your father what you were up to."

"But what were *you* doing down there, Mrs. St. John?" George asked. He still couldn't get over being *right* about this.

"Well, it's a strange story and a sad one." She shook her head. "It all started when the police first stopped by our shop about a month ago."

The St. Johns ran a little electronics shop in Midtown. They sold things like radios and televisions and digital cameras, and Mr. St. John did repairs on stuff that wasn't too complicated.

"They said they had gotten a report that we were selling *stolen goods.* 'Impossible!' I told the police. I mean, can you imagine? Mr. St. John and me, dealing in stolen electronics? But the authorities looked at our inventory and checked the serial numbers and found that actually, a portion of our merchandise had come from a batch of goods they'd traced back to a warehouse robbery over in Brooklyn. Well." Mrs. St. John frowned. "I didn't know *what* to think. After the police left, we checked our records, because I've known all of our vendors personally for years, and finally we figured out who the stolen merchandise was coming from. I have to tell you, it was quite a shock."

George and his friends were leaning forward in anticipation.

"Who?" Derrick blurted out.

"Well . . ." Mrs. St. John looked hesitant. "I'm almost entirely certain of the culprit, but I feel awkward telling you." She sighed. "Because you know him. You should brace yourselves, George and Peter, because it is terribly surprising."

George already knew who it was going to be.

Mrs. St. John took a deep breath and pushed her long, dark hair behind her ear. "It was actually *Mr. Roulain* who sold us those stolen goods," she said. "Our good friend and neighbor."

None of them gasped or cried out. Mrs. St. John looked kind of surprised that they were so unfazed.

"To tell you the truth, Eleanor," George's dad said, "we're actually having our own problems with our good friend Mr. Roulain."

Mrs. St. John raised her eyebrows. "You are? Nothing serious, I hope?"

Peter van Gelder looked at George, who looked at Shannon, Derrick, and Renee. George turned to his dad and shook his head ever so slightly. It didn't make sense to give Mrs. St. John the details about what was going on. Mrs. St. John might want to help them, and then they would be exposing her to danger. . . . It was better just to handle it themselves.

"Well . . ." George's dad said. "No, it's nothing serious."

Mrs. St. John frowned, like she didn't quite believe them. "You know, I never got a great feeling from him. He wasn't very open, but I *never* expected him to be a criminal!"

"I know what you mean, Eleanor," Mr. van Gelder said. "Believe me. But how did you end up in the tunnels?"

"Right. The tunnels," she said. "Well, it *is* kind of a roundabout story.

"I didn't go to the police right away with Roulain's name. I had a hard time believing it was *really* his doing. So I decided to do a little investigating of my own. I had already placed another order with him, and I didn't cancel it. I let him make his delivery." She paused to glance at five eager faces. "Are you sure I can't get anyone something to drink?"

"Not at all, Eleanor. I think we're just anxious to hear this story," George's dad said.

"Of course. So after Roulain's deliverymen dropped off the load of merchandise, I followed them."

"Didn't they notice you behind them?" George asked.

Mrs. St. John grinned. "Not at all, George, because I put on a *blond* wig. I just got in a cab with the wig and said, 'Follow that truck!'"

"Really?" George's father asked.

Mrs. St. John smiled. "Yes, I felt like I was in a movie. And I'm just getting to the good part. I followed the men in the cab, and only a few blocks from here they pulled over and stopped and went into the back of the van. They stayed back there for a bit and then climbed back into the front. That's when I noticed that they were wearing these blue jumpsuits—almost like a mechanic or an electrician would wear. And then I looked closer, and I realized that they had 'Con Edison' embroidered on the chest. I couldn't believe it! These men were trying to pose as electric-company employees!"

"Mr. Roulain used to work for Con Edison, didn't he, Dad?" George looked over at his father.

"That's right," Peter van Gelder agreed. "He must have gotten the jumpsuits from his contacts there."

"And *then*!" Mrs. St. John continued. "I saw the guy in the passenger's seat roll down his window and stick a big Con Edison logo magnet to the side of the truck door!"

George nodded slowly. It all made sense. He had been wondering how Roulain and his guys got all those electronics in and out of the tunnels. The stuff was stashed far from the elevator that marked the underground entrance to Roulain's apartment. Roulain probably kept the stuff away from his apartment to protect himself from being connected to it if they got caught.

"Then they parked the van down by Hudson River Park and walked over to a grating in the side of a hill. While I watched, one of the men pushed a latch and the grating swung open. Then the two of them went inside and started carrying boxes covered with tarps through the grating to the van—stolen electronics equipment, no doubt! All of this in broad daylight!" Mrs. St. John's eyes widened. "So then I realized that Mr. Roulain was storing mysterious electronics *underground*. But I still didn't have proof that they were stolen."

George wondered what he would have done in Mrs. St. John's situation: Would he have been brave enough to have followed Roulain's workers in the first place? Those men were pretty big and scary. George had to hand it to his neighbor: She had guts.

"So," Mrs. St. John continued, "after they left, I headed home to change and grab a camera. I dressed all in black so I could easily blend into the shadows. Then I grabbed a flashlight and headed back to the grate I'd seen the men enter. Fortunately, the park was fairly empty. When no one was looking, I pressed on the grate just like I'd seen Roulain's men do, and it opened right up! I walked straight into that tunnel and didn't look back." Then her smile faded, and Mrs. St. John seemed to get serious. "Kids, if you've been in those tunnels, you know what's going on down there." George and his friends nodded, and she went on. "Peter, there are homeless people living down there, with no other place to go. I tried to talk to them, but they're very scared of strangers. On my second trip down there, I brought some food, and I convinced a couple of the women to talk to me. You wouldn't believe it—they told me they've been forced to find a new home. Some man named Leroy is making them leave the tunnels."

Peter van Gelder and the four kids nodded.
"Eleanor—"

Mrs. St. John looked at George's dad, almost as
if she hadn't heard him. "And I have this horrible
suspicion. I've been trying to convince myself otherwise. I didn't want to believe anyone could be so
cruel, but . . ."

George's dad reached out and put his hand on
Mrs. St. John's arm. "Eleanor, it's Roulain. Roulain
is Leroy."

"*Oh.*" Mrs. St. John shook her head in disgust.
"Well, I guess I have no choice. I have an appoint-
ment with Sergeant Marshall from the Second
Precinct later today. I'm going to tell him all about
Roulain. I can direct him to the stashes of electronics in the tunnels. There were other things, too—
art, jewelry, things you couldn't even imagine."

George's dad put up his hands to stop her.
"Wait a minute, Eleanor. This may be a lot to ask,
but we'd like to hold off on calling the police for
now. Like I said, we have to take care of some
things with Roulain, and we don't want to involve
the authorities until we have that worked out."

Nicely put, Dad, George thought admiringly.

Mrs. St. John didn't hesitate. "Well, of course
I don't *mind*, Peter. I trust you know what's best. I
hope you're not . . . in any danger."

George glanced quickly at his dad, but Peter didn't even blink. "Oh, no, Eleanor. Just a bit of business we need to settle."

Mrs. St. John nodded. "Well, all right. But if you need anything from me, if I can help in any way, just call me. You're like family, you van Gelders." She glanced at George and smiled.

"Thanks, Mrs. St. John. We'll remember that," George said. But he hoped they wouldn't have to give her a call.

Four

The Last Clue

Mrs. St. John wouldn't let them leave through the front door for fear Roulain was spying on them. Instead she made them go out the back door, climb a ladder, and shimmy down the fence between the two yards. As he waited his turn, George sighed. What a terrible day. Just that morning at school he had convinced the group to continue looking for the treasure. He had been sure they were close to claiming it as their own. Now the adventure was continuing, but they were no longer in control. Even if they found the diamond, they'd have to give it away. *But we* will *find the diamond. I'm sure we will,* George thought.

All they had to do was figure out where it was.

"All right," Peter van Gelder said as the whole crew settled back in the kitchen. "Now we know you didn't see Kira lurking in the tunnels, which leads me to believe that she's *not* working for Roulain. Which means we need to start looking for that diamond."

"Right," Shannon agreed. "What I don't get is why Roulain *wants* the diamond that badly. You said that it's probably only worth about a million dollars. Right, Mr. van Gelder? I bet he's spent more than that just buying all the equipment."

"That's true," George's dad said. "Well, here's what I know. There are two groups of people that would be looking for the diamond and might be willing to pay a lot for it. One is the current government of Litaria, which is very corrupt—they're on the United Nations' list of the worst human-rights violators in the world."

"That doesn't sound good," Shannon said.

"It's not. It means the government is oppressing the people by denying them basic freedoms. They're putting people in jail for disagreeing with the leaders. They've ordered the military to attack people who try to speak out against the government."

"That sounds awful," Renee said. "So what does all this have to do with the diamond?"

"Well, there's a small band of revolutionaries that are beginning to organize against the government, and they're gaining more and more followers. The Litarian dictatorship is beginning to worry. I believe they want to find the diamond and destroy it."

Derrick's eyes widened. "Why?" he asked. "I mean, it's this national heirloom, right? Why would they want it destroyed?"

Peter van Gelder sighed. "It all has to do with their fear of being overthrown. As it is, the people of Litaria never accepted the present leader. I think the current regime believes that if the diamond were found and somehow fell into the hands of the revolutionaries, the people of Litaria would completely turn on their current leader. And that would mean the end of his rule."

"Wow, so the revolutionaries probably want the diamond, too," George said.

"That's right, son. Exactly. The revolutionary army is called the Litarian Liberation Army, and if they got ahold of the Eye, they would return it to the royal family. The Litarians' belief in the Eye of Eternity is so great, they would almost certainly fight to overthrow the current government and reinstate the monarchy."

"So would Roulain sell the diamond to one of them?" Shannon asked.

Suddenly Derrick's face lit up. "Wait! I saw a letter on Roulain's desk—it had the official seal of the Litarian government on it."

"Really?" George's dad said. "When did you see this?"

"During Operation: Mapsnatch," Derrick explained. "I snuck into Roulain's apartment to find the fourth piece of the map. I found it and I memorized it, and as I was leaving, I saw the letter on his desk."

"Do you have any idea what it said?" George's dad asked excitedly.

"Sure," said Derrick proudly, "I know exactly what it said." He puffed out his chest a little and grinned. George's dad looked at the rest of them questioningly.

"Derrick has a photographic memory," Shannon said finally. "He can remember anything, even if he only sees it once."

"Oh, right," Peter van Gelder murmured. "That's very fortunate for us. What did the letter say?"

"Let's see." Derrick furrowed his brow in concentration. "It said:

October 16

Dear Mr. Roulain,

This letter is to inform you that we plan to abandon our contract with you if we do not have delivery of the product in the next fourteen days—i.e., by October 30. You have exceeded by more than six months the deadline originally specified in our agreement. Once our relationship is terminated, you will be expected to return the money you were given as an advance, and you will not receive any further payment for the delivery. Please let us know immediately what your intentions are in this regard.

"And it was signed, 'Sincerely, Mikhail Zoloc, Minister of Internal Affairs, Litaria,'" Derrick finished.

Mr. van Gelder shook his head in awe of Derrick's talent, but there was no time to linger in amazement. They had to get this thing figured out.

"What's today?" Shannon asked.

Derrick looked at his watch. "October twenty-eighth."

"Aha," Mr. van Gelder said. "No wonder Roulain is working so hard to find the diamond— and taking such big risks. He's under the gun." He sighed. "The Litarian government is very rich with new oil money. I'm sure they're offering to pay him at least ten times what the diamond is worth. It would be priceless to them politically." Mr. van Gelder looked around at all of them. "All right, kids. Our time is running short, and I believe that Kira is in grave danger. Our mission is to *find that diamond.*"

"Right," Renee said. "Let's look at the maps and try to decipher the clues."

Everyone turned their attention to the maps, which were still carefully arranged on the kitchen table. Again George felt a tingle go up his spine as he realized that they finally had *all four maps* in one place! He let his eyes run over the circular path. The third map matched up perfectly with maps two and four. It had a "III" in the upper-right corner and a wavy tunnel that led through a small room—*That must be the room where we saw Gomes and Leroy's other goons*, George thought—and a compass rose was drawn in the lower-right corner.

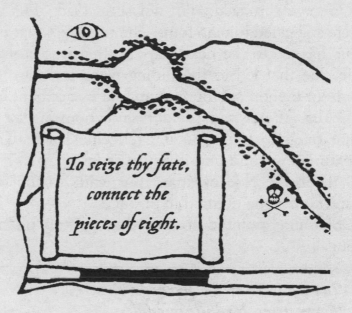

George took a deep breath. According to Kidd's journal, they had everything they needed to find the treasure. *Everything we need to find the Eye of Eternity!*

"This is the new map, right?" George's dad asked, pointing to map three.

"That's right," said Renee.

George's dad pointed to the clue on map three:

To seize thy fate, connect the pieces of eight.

"What do you think that means?"

George shrugged. "I'm not sure, Dad." His eyes were still glued to map four. "The thing is, so far each clue has led to the next map. So that was probably the clue that led to the hiding place for map four. But our friend Paul found map four by accident."

"Aha," Peter van Gelder said, pointing to the clue on map four. "So if each clue leads to the next map . . . and map four is the *last* map . . ."

"Then the clue on map four leads to the treasure!" everyone chimed in at once.

Shannon pointed to the clue written on map four.

Twenty stout men a pyrate crewe be
Forty arms, for sails to haul
Forty eyes, to watch for all
But 'tis their feet ye will need
To go from the mast's base to its peak
If the true meaning of my treasure ye seek

"Figures," Derrick muttered. "It *would* be the longest clue."

"Any ideas, you guys?" George asked, looking around the table. "I'm not sure what it means. I just know he wasn't much of a poet."

"I guess we're looking for a mast," Renee said. "Remember when we saw that tall log on our way to the underground lake, Derrick?" Renee glanced over her shoulder to Derrick, who nodded. George remembered them talking about a mast they'd seen somewhere in the tunnels . . . it was about fifteen feet long, jutting straight out of the tunnel floor.

"Yeah. That could have been a mast, but Roulain's goons were all over it. They'd dug up every single piece of tunnel around, from ten feet away to fifty or sixty."

George's face went pale. "He has this same clue. You think he's found the diamond?"

Derrick sighed and shook his head. "I really don't, George. They set off the booby trap right next to that log. Most of the tunnel floor caved in. And now Roulain wants the diamond from us . . . which means it couldn't have been there."

"I think Derrick's right," Shannon spoke up. "Maybe the mast Roulain found was a decoy. Maybe there's another one that we should be looking for."

George frowned. He felt like his head was going to explode if he tried to concentrate any harder. "So . . . where else could a mast be down there?"

Derrick shrugged. "I dunno. I'm stumped."

They all sat in silence for a minute. George dropped his chin into his hands, too frustrated to think. They had everything they needed right in front of them. So *why* didn't the clue make sense?

Then suddenly Renee's eyes lit up.

"*Stumped!*" She jumped up from the table with a huge grin. "That stump—the one right below the basement entrance! You guys know—we always wonder how it got there. I bet it was Kidd."

George smacked his hand on the table. "Of course! There was that engraving on it. 'Campbell's Yard'! That could be a shipyard or something!"

George could feel his heart pounding. He looked around at his friends, excitement shining in all of their eyes. Finally, a lead! This was it! They were so close!

"Well, let's not waste any more time!" Shannon said, jumping out of her seat. "Let's get down there and dig up our diamond!"

George's dad hesitated. "Do we really need to go down? Into the tunnels with the booby traps and the goons?" He didn't look too excited.

"Yeah, down there," said Shannon. "Wait till you see it, Mr. van Gelder. You'll be amazed."

George's dad slowly pushed back his chair and stood up, a little smile forming on his face. "Yes, I'm sure I will be. If I make it down there."

"Oh, we'll get you down there, Mr. van Gelder," Derrick said with a big grin. "And bring a shovel! We've got some digging to do!"

Five

FORTY FEET

Once again George, his dad, and his friends trooped down the narrow basement stairs and headed for the tiny room with the trapdoor, but this time they had a new sense of purpose. They had moved the boxes of books earlier, so they were able to walk straight to the door and open it.

Renee went over to where they stashed their equipment, under a bench in a dark corner. There was a lot of stuff: harnesses and ropes for getting in and out of the tunnels from the basement, helmets, headlamps, plus a whole bunch of tools that they had collected for different reasons along the way. Last of all, Renee dragged out two shovels. She looked at the assembled crew and grinned.

"All *right*," said Derrick, grabbing a helmet and strapping it on. "Let's get going."

Shannon and George grabbed their harnesses and started to gear up.

"I'm going to fit Mr. van Gelder with a harness and help him down," said Renee. "Once you're ready, you guys can go ahead, and then you'll pass a harness back up to me when he's at the bottom."

As Renee adjusted the harness buckles to fit an adult, Mr. van Gelder started talking—almost to himself. "I was going to build bookshelves, remember, for all these books?" he said. "If I had done that, I would have found the door."

"Yeah, I remember that. We were going to have to come up with something if you actually got them built," George said.

"Well, I would have, but I could never find the screws and braces that came with them," George's dad said. "It drove me crazy!"

George bit his lip and looked away. Actually, he had stolen those screws and braces and hidden them in his desk drawer to delay his dad's project. He wondered whether he should come clean now but decided against it. They didn't have much time to argue. They had a diamond to find and a Litarian to rescue!

In order to get down to the tunnels, they had to navigate the long drop. The kids had set up a rope using Renee's parents' caving equipment at the beginning of the adventure, and they'd all learned how to rappel down into the tunnel.

George's dad watched as each kid in turn walked to the edge of the drop, clipped the rope onto their harness, and jumped into the dark hole. His eyes got wider and wider.

"Ummm . . . Renee?" he said finally. "I'm really not sure about this. I may be too old or too heavy. Actually, I may be too scared. Maybe I should just let you all go on down—"

Renee patted him on the shoulder. "It's okay, Mr. van Gelder, I'll walk you through it. It looks a lot harder than it is." She held out the harness. "Just step into this . . . and buckle it there."

George listened from below as his dad got his harness all set up. "Here we go, Mr. van Gelder. No time to spare," Renee said in a reassuring voice as she hurried him over to the trapdoor. George figured Renee wanted to get him down quickly before he lost his nerve. He looked toward the light spilling from the basement and saw his dad's head peek over the edge.

"Okay, so I just step into this dark hole and trust that this thing is going to hold me?" George heard his dad ask. His voice made it sound like a joke.

"Oh, it'll hold you, sir, there's no question about that. Just keep a firm grip on the rope so you don't slide down too fast." Renee smiled encouragingly.

He stood at the edge, and George thought it looked like there was no way he was ever going to move. But Renee had had a lot of experience rappelling and she knew how to handle the situation. She began to gently push George's dad toward the edge.

"Oh, wait! Not quite yet, I just need another moment—"

"It's okay, Mr. van Gelder," Renee said, all the while gently pushing, "down you go . . . no worries." She spoke in a soothing tone, and Peter van Gelder dropped off the edge with a small cry. But the relay device soon stopped him, and he just swung in midair, not going anywhere because he had a death grip on the rope.

"Now just ease up on that rope a little, Mr. van Gelder," Renee said.

He did and dropped a few feet with a jerk, slamming to a halt as he cranked down on the rope again.

George couldn't help being kind of impressed by his father. He could see that his dad was royally freaked out. And why shouldn't he be? His dad was a historian—made for sipping tea and reading big, moldy texts in his tweed vests and glasses. He wasn't made to be an adventurer. He didn't even like climbing up on ladders.

"You can do it, Dad," George called. He stepped backward and almost tripped over a stump—the stump that could be the mast in the clue. It was almost directly underneath the hole, just a plain old log that looked a lot like a tree stump. But a few weeks ago George had studied the log and found an engraving on it:

CAMPBELL'S YARD
BOSTON, MASSACHUSETTS
1683

George heard a *thunk* and turned back to his friends. Shannon and Derrick were patting his dad on the back and helping him unbuckle his harness.

"Hey, you made it, Dad!" George said happily. He walked over to help his friends with the harness, and together they got it off and tied it to the rope for Renee to pull up.

"That was . . . very interesting," George's dad said thoughtfully. He looked at George with a funny expression. "George, I had no idea you were lowering yourself down here that way. You must be very . . . brave."

George couldn't believe he was hearing this. "Thanks, Dad," he replied, glancing up as Renee retrieved the harness and suited herself up. "You're brave, too."

George's dad chuckled. "I suppose so, son. When I have to be." He watched in awe as Renee stepped over the edge and zipped down the rope in three seconds, then expertly unhooked her harness.

"Good job, Mr. van Gelder," she told George's dad with another smile. "Rappelling down a rope can be scary the first time, especially in the dark, but you did a great job."

George thought his dad blushed just a little. "Thank you, Renee. You're quite the capable coach."

Renee grinned.

George stepped aside and pointed to the log. "Well, here it is, you guys."

Derrick, Shannon, Renee, and George's dad all gathered around and examined it.

"I'm starting to get excited. It seemed crazy at first, but I think that this might actually be what Kidd was talking about!" Shannon said.

"I know," Derrick said. "I can't believe I never thought much of this thing before. I thought it was just a moldy old log left over from building the subway. But of course Kidd would have had to have put it here—what kind of tree grows down here in the dark?"

"The clue said, 'Forty eyes, to watch for all, but 'tis their feet ye will need.' So I suppose forty feet from here is where we need to look," George's dad said. He looked around, frowning this way and that. "Where should we start? I can barely see down here."

"Renee has a special sonic range-finder, so we'll

be able to measure exactly forty feet," George told him.

"Sounds like a plan, guys!" Shannon said. "Now, let's get to work!"

Renee got out the range-finder, and they decided to send Derrick to be the forty-foot mark. There were really only two tunnels that extended forty feet from the mast. One was in the direction of the abandoned subway station. They'd try that one first. Renee held the device and trained the signal on Derrick.

"Okay, you're at thirty-four feet," she called to him. "Keep going!"

"All right!" Derrick called back.

A few seconds later Renee called to him again. "Right there!" She flashed George a big grin and then ran to follow Derrick. "That's forty feet! Let's go!"

George glanced over at his dad and Shannon, then eagerly galloped down the tunnel after Renee. "Grab the shovel, Dad!" he called behind him. "Get ready to dig up our diamond!"

Derrick was standing motionless in the middle of the narrow tunnel, his feet submerged in the few inches of flowing water that covered the dirt floor. Soon George, Renee, Shannon, and Peter van Gelder had surrounded him.

"All right, Derrick," George's dad said with a

smile, holding up the shovel. "Step aside, and we'll dig up this treasure!"

Derrick stepped to the side as George's dad moved closer and thrust the shovel into the tunnel floor. It only went an inch or two before it stopped with a sudden *thunk!* George's dad shook a little from the vibration of the shovel.

"What the heck . . . ?" he murmured.

George glanced at each of his three friends. All of their faces reflected one feeling: worry. "Try again, Dad," George urged.

"All right," Peter van Gelder said. He raised the shovel and once again brought it down through the tunnel floor, this time a few inches from where he'd struck before. Again the shovel slammed into something solid under only an inch or so of dirt. "I'll be darned," George's dad muttered. He leaned closer and gently brushed some loose dirt from the tunnel floor. "George, shine your helmet light right here."

George took off his helmet and angled the light down at the ground. Beneath the dirt his dad had moved, there was something gray with little sparkles. . . .

"Stone," Derrick said after a moment. He leaned closer. "It looks like solid stone. Can I have the shovel, Mr. van Gelder?"

Wordlessly George's dad handed the shovel to

him. Derrick began to scrape the dirt off the sur-
rounding tunnel floor as quietly as he could. First
he cleared an area of a few inches . . . then about
a square foot. George shot a nervous glance at
Shannon. She looked about as worried as he was
feeling. After a few minutes Derrick had cleared
about a square yard of tunnel floor. Beneath their
feet was nothing but solid, impenetrable stone.

George's dad rubbed his eyes. "It looks like
granite," he said. "I hate to say this, kids, but the
diamond can't be here. There's no way we can dig
through solid granite."

Shannon sighed. "I believe you, Mr. van Gelder,
but is there any way this *could* be it? I mean,
maybe this stone is one big piece that was moved
here after Captain Kidd's day? Maybe we can
move it and dig underneath?"

George's dad shook his head. "I'm sorry. But it
looks like this is much bigger than one movable
piece. It looks pretty solid. I would imagine it runs
most of the length of this tunnel. And I do believe
it was here in Captain Kidd's day. That would
explain why the tunnel's ceiling is so low—because
he couldn't drill through the granite floor."

George frowned. "Well, let's try the other direction," he said. "We still have time, guys—let's get
moving on finding that diamond."

Silently George, his friends, and his father headed back up the tunnel to where the log was standing. They felt a little less hopeful now. Peter van Gelder glanced down the tunnel in the other direction. It didn't seem to go very far.

"I don't know if that's forty feet before it hits the wall," Mr. van Gelder said. George knew his dad was really good at measuring distances by eye, but he hoped he was wrong this time.

"Well, it has to be, Dad. Otherwise we're back to square one."

Renee, standing right on top of the log, sent Derrick off the other way with her signal on him. Just as Peter predicted, he soon hit the wall.

"You're only at twenty-nine feet, Derrick!" Renee said, dismayed.

"Well, what do you want me to do? Walk right through the wall?" Derrick snapped. George could tell that stress and disappointment were getting to them.

For a few seconds they all just stared glumly at the log or mast or whatever it was supposed to be.

"Now what?" Derrick asked sullenly. "We can't dig in one direction, and we can't get far enough in the other. Some clue!"

Shannon frowned. "Do you think the mast is another decoy?" she asked.

"It's possible," George said carefully. "But it seems

kind of cruel of Captain Kidd to have *two* decoys."

"Well, it wouldn't surprise me. He *wasn't* a nice guy, George," Shannon said. "He used skeletons as part of his treasure hunt, and he killed Sergei Trenov and buried him in these tunnels!"

"You don't know that!" George cried.

"Shhh," Renee whispered. "Guys, calm down. We don't want Roulain's goons to figure out that we're down here."

George looked down at the ground and sighed. This seemed like the longest day of his life. And it was only what, four, five o'clock in the afternoon? The truth was, he didn't know why he was defending Captain Kidd. If the pirate had been in front of him right at that moment, George would have liked to have given him a piece of his mind, to have told him that he'd been unfair. George wanted to scream. *Why did you have to make this so hard?*

"Hello?"

Everyone froze at the sound of a new voice. It was coming from farther down the tunnels, in the direction that led to the abandoned subway station. A split second after they heard the voice, George caught Renee's eye, and he could see what she was thinking: *Way to go, George! Someone heard us!*

But as the sound echoed off the tunnel walls, George recognized it. Relief flooded through his body. "Paul?" he called down the tunnel.

For a while everyone was silent. The only sound was the *sploosh . . . sploosh* of footsteps in the shallow water that had collected on the tunnel floor. Then George spotted their friend Paul stepping into the light of his miner's helmet.

"Hey, Paul. What's up?" George greeted him.

Paul squinted against the light and turned away. "Turn off the bright. Please?"

George picked up his helmet and pointed the light at the far wall, taking the beam off Paul's face. "Is that okay? We need a little light to see down here."

Paul slowly turned back to George, still squinting. "Okay."

Then nobody said anything for what was probably only a few seconds but seemed to George like a half hour. George's dad walked over and looked nervously from George to Paul. Paul's eyes widened when he saw George's dad, and he took a few rigid steps backward. He looked so frightened, George worried for a second that he was going to run back down the tunnel and out of sight.

"Hey, Paul," George said quickly, smiling encouragingly, "this is my dad. Dad, this is Paul— he's been helping us get around the tunnels."

George's dad smiled, but Paul's frightened expression remained.

"It's a pleasure to meet you, Paul," George's dad said warmly. "I'm Peter van Gelder. Thank you for helping my son and his friends stay out of trouble."

Derrick laughed. "Paul did try to keep us out of trouble, Mr. van Gelder," he said, walking over to Paul with a smile. "He warned us to stay out of the tunnels, but we kept coming back."

Paul looked from Derrick to George's dad, still seeming uncertain. "Why are you here?" he asked finally, ignoring George's dad and turning to Derrick. "I saw your brights and I heard you yelling. But you didn't come get me."

Shannon rushed over and put her hand on Paul's shoulder. "Hey, Paul," she said. "I'm sorry we didn't try to find you. Something's happened that made this all much more serious. That's why George's dad came down with us this time." She looked over at Peter van Gelder, and Paul warily followed her gaze.

"The thing is, Paul," George's dad said gently, "a good friend of mine was kidnapped. I got a note signed by a 'Leroy.'"

Paul's eyes widened.

"Leroy is making us exchange our friend for the diamond," George's dad explained, "but we don't have the diamond yet. So we have to try to find it fast, or we have to figure out another way to save Kira."

George's dad looked at the floor. George thought

his dad seemed to get a little sadder every time they mentioned Kira's name. He must really be worried about her.

"Oh," Paul said. He looked from Shannon to George to Derrick. "So you're looking for the diamond now?"

"Yeah," Derrick replied. "But we're not having much luck."

Paul nodded. "Oh."

Nobody said anything for a little while.

"It just doesn't seem *right*," Derrick said after about a minute. "I was so sure we had found the answer." He walked back to the twenty-nine-foot mark. When he got there, he sighed and punched the wall in frustration. "Stupid wall! Stupid Captain Kidd and his stupid clues!"

"*Wait!*" Renee dashed over to where Derrick stood. "Guys, did you hear that?" She looked from George, to his dad, to Shannon. They all looked back blankly. "Derrick, punch the wall again."

Derrick looked at Renee like she was nuts but gamely raised his fist and punched the wall once more.

Renee listened as he punched. And then her eyes lit up and she nodded. "Did you hear that? There's still hope." She walked back toward the stump with a big smile on her face. "The wall is *hollow*! That means the diamond is behind it!"

George was feeling so down, it took him a minute to figure out what Renee was saying.

"Well, it looks pretty solid. How will we get through it?" Peter van Gelder asked.

Renee was already buckling herself back into her harness. "We can use a pickax. It's in with the spelunking equipment I have upstairs. I'll run and get it."

Before anybody could say anything to stop her, Renee was already zipping up the rope and into the van Gelders' basement. "Be right back!" she called down.

George, Shannon, Derrick, and George's dad looked at each other in confusion.

"What happened? What did she mean?" Paul asked suddenly.

George looked over. "Well, we think the treasure must be forty feet from this log right here. But when we measured forty feet in each direction, it just didn't work." Slowly, as if he were moving through water, George wandered over to the wall where Derrick stood. He thumped a few times on the wall himself. Sure enough, a hollow sound rang out. "But this wall is hollow, so that means the diamond could be behind here. In Captain Kidd's time there might not have been a wall at all. He might even have built the wall to hide the treasure."

Paul walked over and pressed his hand against the wall. "The diamond might be in there?"

"Yeah." George could feel the corners of his mouth turning up.

Derrick was beginning to smile, too. "All *right*."

As the crew gathered around the twenty-nine-foot mark, Renee zipped down the rope again, this time carrying a small pickax.

"Usually you use this to climb rocks," she said as she unclipped herself. "But I think it will work just fine for getting through tunnel walls!"

Renee walked over to the rest of them, holding the pickax high. "We can take turns," she said. "But we should probably start with the strongest person. I think that'd be you, Mr. van Gelder."

George's dad looked a little flustered. "Well, I'd be happy to, Renee."

Renee showed George's father how to hold the pickax, and slowly, steadily, Mr. van Gelder began to chip away at the wall. After the first blow George could see that the wall wasn't all that hard—it was mostly packed dirt, not solid rock like he'd feared, which meant they actually had a shot of getting to the other side tonight.

After a few minutes the pickax began to make a different sound as it drove into the wall. Peter van Gelder pulled the ax out with a great effort and

sighed. George could see that his dad was working hard and getting sweaty—but he hadn't asked
anyone else to step in yet.

"We've hit cement," George's dad said as he
examined the wall. "That means we're getting to
something man-made. And relatively recent. Kidd
didn't build this wall."

George's heart sank. If this wall was recent, did
that mean the diamond had already been dug up
whenever the wall had been built?

After they hit the cement, their progress slowed
down a little bit. George's mind was so clouded
with frustration and diamond fever that he couldn't
tell whether it had been five minutes or thirty
before his dad struck a blow that connected with a
funny *tchunk*. Everyone jumped up, and George's
father pulled the pickax back and peered into the
hole he had created. By now they had dug about a
foot into the wall.

"That's it," Peter van Gelder said. "Kids, we've
hit the other side."

Shannon leaned in and tried to peer through
the hole herself. "What's in there?"

"It's too dark to see anything," George's dad
replied. "But let me keep digging. We need a hole
big enough to climb through."

To George, time seemed to slow down as his dad

struggled to enlarge the hole. First the hole was the size of a baseball, then the size of a basketball. It was still too dark in there to see what was inside. Finally, what seemed like years after they'd started, the hole was big enough for them to climb through.

Peter van Gelder threw down the pickax and wiped his forehead with his shirtsleeve. "Well," he said, rolling up his sleeves and grinning at George and his friends, "shall we, team?"

George looked at Renee, Shannon, Derrick, and Paul. All of them looked excited but also a little hesitant. George knew how they must be feeling. It wasn't that he was scared of what was on the other side—they had seen some horrifying things over the past few weeks, and they'd survived them all. What frightened George more was being so close to the diamond. In just a few minutes their whole adventure might be over. George wasn't sure how he felt about that.

It was Derrick who snapped him back to reality. "All *right!*" he cried, throwing a leg up over the bottom edge of the hole. "Let's get that diamond!"

"Everyone turn off your helmet brights," Shannon suggested as she clicked hers off. "That way when we all get inside, we can all turn on our lights at the same time and find the diamond together." She shot a quick glance at Paul and smiled. "We'll muffle our brights, of course, so we don't hurt anyone's eyes."

The corners of Paul's mouth turned up just a little. It wasn't quite a smile, but for Paul, it was close enough.

One by one, Derrick, Renee, Paul, Shannon, and George squeezed through the hole and into the musty darkness beyond. Once through the opening, George slipped several feet down to the floor of this new room, which was lower than the floor of the tunnels. He looked all around him, but it was so dark that he couldn't see his hand in front of his face, much less anything else. He could only see behind him, where his dad was struggling to squeeze through the narrow opening.

"Take my arm, Dad," George offered, reaching for his dad's hand. "Be careful, there's a little drop."

"Urrrrgh," Peter van Gelder moaned as he pulled one foot, then the other, up onto the lip of the opening. "This is a tight fit." Holding on to George, he slowly squeezed through and let his feet drop down to the lower floor. As George's dad stepped farther away from the opening, George could no longer see his expression. "Goodness, it's dark in here," his dad said, reaching down to retrieve his miner's helmet from the ground. "Well, kids," he said, lifting the helmet and placing his finger on the light switch, "shall we turn on our lights and see what we have here?"

Everyone except Paul reached for the switch on his or her helmet.

"Remember, though," Shannon said, "hold your hand in front of your lamp so it isn't too bright."

Click. All of the helmet lights switched on.

George blinked and looked all around him. It took his eyes a minute to adjust to the filtered light. He sucked in his breath. Then he caught Derrick and Shannon's eyes, and all of his friends opened their mouths at the same time.

"Whoooooooaaaa!"

Six

WINDSOR STATION

George felt a tingle run down his spine. This was amazing. Nothing he'd imagined had prepared him for this!

"I don't believe it!" Renee cried. "Why is this all the way down in the tunnels?"

The room where George and his friends were standing was like something out of an ancient mansion. There was a long-empty fountain standing in a corner, and dusty chandeliers hung from the ceiling. The walls were covered with delicate, faded paintings of landscapes and cherubs, and there were two windows covered by thick, expensive-looking maroon curtains. An elegant staircase led up toward what must have once been an exit but was now just a boarded-up doorway. George turned his head and spied a dusty grand piano and grandfather clock sitting in a corner of the room. *Where are we?* he wondered. *Have we broken into the basement of some millionaire's dusty old mansion?*

Then suddenly George had a thought. "Do you think . . ." he began, craning his neck to look all around the room. Derrick, Shannon, and Renee all looked at him curiously.

"What, George?" Shannon asked finally. "What do you think this is?"

George scrunched up his eyebrows, trying to find proof of what he was thinking. "I think maybe this might be some kind of secret underground lair," he said. "For Captain Kidd!"

"Hmmm," Renee murmured. Peter van Gelder looked curious and began to walk around the room.

"I don't think this is from the right time period, George," he said mildly. "The cement in the walls and the floors, for one. And everything down here is too perfectly preserved. It feels too new—and the style isn't quite seventeenth century."

George frowned. If they weren't in Captain Kidd's lair, where *were* they?

"Where do these go?" Derrick asked, walking over to a short staircase. The stairs led down, but the room was so dark that all George could see at the bottom of the stairs was blackness. The staircase had seen better days, too—like the stairs leading up, it was elegantly carved and carpeted, but the railings had caved in on one side and one of the stairs was broken. Derrick stood on the top step and slowly started to make his way down. But George's dad stopped him.

"Wait!" he called, running over to the top of the

stairs. "We don't know if these stairs are stable. They might collapse under your weight."

Derrick frowned and peered into the darkness below. "Awww. I'll be really careful."

George's dad shook his head and shone his light down the staircase to see what lay ahead. From where he stood, George could see a dark platform, about six steps down from the room where they stood now. But beyond that—George blinked.

"Is that a *train car*?" George gasped, running over to his dad's side. Renee, Shannon, and Paul drew closer, too, Renee wearing an expression of pure fascination. They were looking at the front of what appeared to be a tiny subway car—about three-fourths the length of the ones they rode almost every day. But on closer inspection, George realized that there were some other differences between this train car and the subways he was used to. It was round, for one—a perfect cylinder about eight feet in diameter. And it was wooden, like the old-fashioned subway cars from the thirties that George had seen on his class trip to the Transit Museum. George's dad was still shining his light around the carpeted platform. His helmet lamp reflected off two bronze statues on either side of the train doors. Each statue was of a young man holding a cluster of what must have been colored lights.

"That's Mercury," George's dad said in a low voice.

"Messenger of the gods and a symbol of speed."

"What are we *looking* at?" Derrick's voice sounded next to George. "And more important, where's the diamond?"

Renee squeezed past George so that she was standing next to him at the top of the staircase. "I think I can answer your first question," she said, angling her helmet light so that it illuminated a sign above the train car, etched on the tunnel's header.

WINDSOR STATION
PNEUMATIC (1870) SUBWAY

"Puh-nee-matic subway?" Shannon said, frowning up at the sign. "What the heck is that?"

Renee shook her head in amazement. "*New*-matic. I really don't believe we found this. There are only two stations like this, and one was wrecked when they built the City Hall subway station." She looked at the rest of them and smiled. "I read all about this in *New York Underground*. Back in the 1860s, this guy named Alfred Ely Beach decided that the way to move people in the city was underground—making the streets less crowded and safer to walk on."

George nodded. "That makes sense. But isn't that what the regular subway does?"

"Yeah, but this was 1870—at least thirty years before the subway we know got built," Renee explained. "Beach came up with a plan to move train cars through underground tunnels with huge, ten-foot fans at either end of the tunnel. But the mayor at the time didn't want it. So Alfred Ely Beach rented the basement of a clothing store on Broadway and started digging his tunnels at night—in total secret."

"Whoa," muttered Shannon. "What did they do with all the dirt?"

"They piled it into wagons with muffled wheels and dumped it outside the city," Renee said. "You'd never think they'd have gotten away with it, but they did. By the time a reporter caught on to the secret tunnel-building, it was all finished. And for a couple of years the pneumatic subway was a huge success. They just didn't have the money to extend it. That's why there were only two stations."

"Crazy," Derrick muttered. "So, um, this is all very interesting, but . . . where's the diamond?"

George looked from Derrick to Shannon to Paul to his dad. They all looked pretty confused.

"Well, it was twenty-nine feet at the opening we cut," Shannon said finally, "so if we measure eleven feet from there . . . in the same direction . . ."

Derrick turned to Renee. "Hey, go stand by the

opening and I'll start walking away again," he said. "You can tell me when I'm at eleven feet, and we'll start digging there."

"Okay," Renee agreed, but she didn't look very enthusiastic. "You know, though, guys . . . they would have had to really tear up the ground to build this station. . . ."

Derrick shook his head like he didn't want to hear any of that. "Let's not talk about any of that yet," he said. "We have to *try*."

Renee nodded and walked back to the opening, and Derrick started backing slowly away. "You still have a few feet," Renee said as Derrick reached the head of the stairs.

Derrick shot a questioning look at George's dad, who sighed. "Just let me go down first," George's dad said finally. "I'll make sure that the stairs are safe."

The ancient wooden steps creaked under Peter van Gelder's weight, but they remained intact until he reached the platform level. "All right," George's dad said. "You can come down, kids. Just be careful."

Slowly Derrick made his way down the stairs and stepped onto the train platform, staring at the tiny car. "Okay, Renee," he said. "Am I there yet?"

"A little farther," she replied.

Derrick backed to the edge of the platform. "Now?" he asked.

Renee shook her head. "That's only thirty-eight feet."

Derrick groaned, and George began to feel a little deflated. "That means it's on the tracks," Derrick said, looking down at the train tracks. "How do we get down there?"

Carefully George went down the creaky staircase, followed by Shannon and Paul. The three of them scanned the area, along with Derrick and George's dad.

"There," Paul said after a moment, pointing to a tiny ironwork ladder a few feet down.

Wordlessly the five of them walked over to the ladder and looked down at the track. George's dad followed and grabbed the ladder by the handrails, giving it a thorough shake. "Seems solid," he said. "And it's only a few feet down. Let's go."

One by one George and his friends climbed down the ladder onto the tracks. George shuddered as he looked down the dark tunnel. He wondered how far it extended—it couldn't be far, since the only other station had been destroyed years ago. *It feels really creepy being down here,* George thought with a frown. He looked around at his friends' faces. *We could be really close,* he thought. *So why don't I feel more excited?*

"Okay, Derrick," Renee called from the opening, "go to the left a couple of feet. No, now go back a little. Take half a step back . . . *there!*" She smiled and ran over to the staircase. "That's forty feet exactly."

"All right, Derrick," George's dad said. "Where's that shovel we brought down? I think it's time for digging."

Renee carefully creaked down the stairs and joined them on the tracks. Derrick produced the shovel and looked at their five eager faces.

"George," Derrick said slowly, "you're our captain. I think you should get to dig."

George smiled. "Hey, thanks, man." He took the shovel from Derrick's hands and looked around at his friends. "Here goes nothing!" He hefted the shovel into the air and then drove it into the ground with as much force as he could muster. The shovel's head dipped into the ground, and George pulled out a rough chunk. "This isn't too hard," George said quietly. "That's good—this shouldn't take too long."

That's what George thought. But half an hour later, with a hole about three feet deep, none of the pyrates had seen any sign of the Eye of Eternity. Not one sign. George could feel sweat trickling down his back, and his arms were dark with grime. He looked at his friends' faces. None of them looked very hopeful anymore.

George paused and stuck the shovel into the ground. He wiped his forehead with his shirtsleeve as he looked down the tracks, thinking: *They would have had to totally tear up the ground to put this system into place. If the Eye of Eternity was here in 1699 . . .*

He didn't want to complete that sentence, even in his head.

"I'll take over for you, George," Shannon offered, grabbing the shovel. She seemed a little too excited, almost like she was forcing it. "I mean, we've got to be really close now, right? Now that you've loosened up all this dirt . . ." Shannon grabbed the shovel's handle and stepped into the hole. Without another word, she started throwing out dirt. For about fifteen minutes they waited as Shannon dug. George's spirits were getting lower and lower. *Be there!* he shouted in his head at the diamond, keeping a sharp eye out for any change in the soil as Shannon brought each shovelful up. *Come on! Just a few more inches! You have to be there!*

"Whoa," Shannon said after a while, wiping the sweat from her face and looking up at the rim of the hole. "We've dug pretty far. Someone else wanna take over?"

There was a pause of a few seconds. George glanced at Derrick and Renee; they looked uncertain and sad.

"I'm sorry to say this," George's dad said finally, "but we've dug pretty far. They would have had to move a tremendous amount of soil to build these tunnels, and most everything that had been here would have been cleared out." He sighed. "It just doesn't seem to be here. I really think the builders either found the diamond or moved it with the soil they hauled away as they were constructing the system."

Shannon's face fell as she climbed out of the hole and then looked back in. "You mean . . . "

Peter van Gelder looked uncomfortably at George and his friends. His expression was full of sympathy and regret. George groaned inwardly; he knew what his dad was going to say, and he hated it. It just didn't seem possible. *Why did we come so far just to get screwed up by a stupid station with a round train?*

"Kids," George's dad said, "I hate to be the one to give up. You've worked so hard to get here and risked so much." He looked right at George and sighed again. "But I think it might be over. If the diamond was here, it seems to be gone now."

George felt his stomach drop all the way to his toes. So this was how their whole adventure was going to end? No diamond—and now no Kira? Nobody made a sound as they stood motionless on the abandoned tracks. George didn't even know what to say next. He felt too miserable to say anything at all.

"What about your friend?" Paul asked. He was looking right at George's dad with a concerned expression.

"What about our treasure hunt?" Shannon echoed, in a much smaller voice.

Peter van Gelder frowned. "Well, first I think we should go back to the house," he said finally. "I know you kids must be disappointed. But we have to think of some way to save Kira *without* the diamond—and unfortunately, I think that means it's time to call the police."

The police? George tried to hide his concern. "Dad," he said, "I really don't think that's a good idea. What if—"

"George, we don't really have many options right now." George's dad cut him off. George could hear the frustration in his father's voice. He knew his dad was trying to hold it together and keep them moving forward, trying the next thing. But he also knew that Roulain had connections with the police. George had heard Roulain's thugs talking about it. Who knew what might happen to his dad if he found a cop who was on Roulain's payroll? Who knew what might happen to any of them?

But more than anything, George knew that calling the police would be the same as calling an end to their whole adventure. They'd be giving up on finding the Eye of Eternity—for good.

George's dad climbed the ladder and headed for the stairs that led back to Captain Kidd's tunnels. "Come on, kids," he said glumly, gesturing to the opening. "Time to go home."

George followed his dad without even looking up. He felt like the whole adventure was self-destructing. The diamond was gone, and his dad was going to call the police, and who knew what Roulain might do—

"*Pssst.*"

George looked up. Shannon was standing next to him, looking strangely excited.

"What?" he asked.

"I have an idea," Shannon whispered. "But your dad will never go for it. We have to get rid of him."

Seven

NEVER GIVE UP

Leaving Paul in the tunnels, the crew reluctantly headed up the basement stairs.

"I need to think this through," George's dad announced, shaking his head. Shannon shot George a Look with a capital *L*. George knew what that Look meant.

Give your dad something to do. We've got to get him out of the house!

"Um, h-hey, Dad," George stammered, grabbing one of the kitchen chairs. "I think—I mean, Shannon and I were talking, and, um, we thought you really—"

George glanced at Shannon, hoping for some assistance. He couldn't help noticing out of the corner of his eye that Derrick was looking at him like he'd lost his mind.

"We thought there must be historical documents that mention the building of the pneumatic subway, right?" Shannon said. George shot her a grateful look. *Perfect!*

George's dad frowned thoughtfully as he turned on the burner under the teakettle. "I suppose," he said. "Though if the whole thing was really built in secret, there wouldn't be newspaper articles and such written while it was being constructed. Anything we find would have been written after the fact."

"Right, but maybe we could find something that mentions where the dirt was taken or how the station was constructed. Anything we could tell Roulain about the diamond could help. Maybe there was a weird chest or trapdoor or something that the subway workers found. I mean, I can't imagine that Kidd would just stick the diamond loose in the ground. Right?" Shannon looked at George's dad hopefully. Even she looked a little confused, like she wasn't sure *what* she was saying. But George's dad was staring off at the refrigerator with a thoughtful expression on his face.

"It does seem odd that the builders would find an extremely valuable diamond and not report it to the press." He glanced at Renee. "Renee, do you remember any mention of strange findings in the book you read? Any obstacles or unexpected discoveries?"

Renee looked even more confused. "Well, they ran into the foundation of an old fort when they were tunneling," she said. "But it didn't really say anything else."

George jumped in and put his hand on his father's shoulder. "The thing is, Dad," he said eagerly, "we know there's no diamond. I mean, we've tried everything we can to find it—and it's just not there. Which means we have to think of some other way to save Kira." George paused, waiting to see his father's reaction. His dad sighed heavily and George continued. "Maybe if we convince Roulain that the diamond's not there, he'll let us have Kira back. I mean, he can't keep holding her forever—especially if we have proof that the Eye of Eternity is gone." George tried to make his face look disappointed. He glanced over at Shannon, who quickly pasted on a pout as well. While his dad was looking at her, George looked at Renee and Derrick and frantically mouthed, *Help! We have to get him out of here!* Derrick nodded his understanding.

"Yeah!" he threw in, still not looking very sure of what he was about to say. "Um, it's too bad that we can't have somebody go do research, like at the library or something. Maybe there's an article or a historic document or something that proves the diamond's not there." Derrick glanced at George as if to say, *Was that good?* George nodded gratefully. *Good job, Derrick.*

Peter van Gelder was sort of staring off into the distance, considering their words. Finally he seemed to come back to life, and he looked at George with a concerned expression. "You kids really believe that Roulain would give us Kira back if we could prove the diamond's gone?" he asked.

George glanced at Shannon, who nodded vigorously. "Yeah," George replied. "I mean, think about it, Dad—as much as Roulain and the Litarian government want the diamond, if it's not there, it's just not there. If Roulain can prove that the diamond's been gone for over a century, maybe the Litarians will let him off the hook and let him keep his money. And either way, he doesn't need Kira."

Peter van Gelder nodded thoughtfully. Just then the teakettle broke in with a shrill whistle. "All right," he said finally. "We'll take a quick trip to the library. Actually, it might be better to check the university archives. It's a fantastic resource for local historical documents. But this is the last straw. If the diamond was found or we hit another dead end, then it's time to call the police."

George shrugged. "All right, Dad," he said. "I still think calling the police is a bad idea, but that sounds fair."

"Good," George's dad said, stepping forward to turn off the burner. The teakettle's whistle dissolved into a *sssss*. George's dad turned from the stove. "I guess there's no time for tea. We need to do this quickly. Let's get going."

Shannon shot George a desperate look. "Um, wait, Dad!" George said, looking around the kitchen. His gaze settled on the phone, and he was hit by a flash of inspiration. "We should probably stay here . . . because Roulain might call," he suggested. "I mean, he could be calling with information about where Kira is at any moment. Or . . . he might decide to call us and change the rules."

Shannon nodded. "I think you should leave us here, Mr. van Gelder," she said. "We can keep studying the maps and see if there's any other possible place for the diamond. And like George said, we can answer the phone if Roulain calls."

Peter van Gelder looked at the pyrate gang and frowned. "I don't know," he said. "I'm not sure I like the idea of leaving you here by yourselves—"

"But actually, we'd probably be safer here!" Renee broke in. "I mean, who knows what could happen out on the streets?"

"Yeah, Roulain could kidnap us and try to torture us for information!" Shannon added.

George looked at his friends in surprise. That idea had never occurred to him. Roulain had already kidnapped him and Shannon once— what would stop him from doing it again?

George shuddered. Maybe it *was* better to stay behind at the house. At least they could lock all the windows and doors and barricade themselves inside.

Peter van Gelder was still frowning, considering. He looked at George and nodded slowly. "I suppose you're right," he said after a minute. "But you must promise not to go out that door," he added, pointing to the front door. "I want you to stay safe and stay by the phone. I'll go to the university archives, and I should be back in an hour. Stay safe."

"We'll try, Mr. van Gelder," Derrick promised. George's dad started for the door. As an afterthought, he came back and gave George a quick hug. "Take care, kids," he said, and then he opened the front door and was gone.

George and his friends waited until his dad had been gone a few minutes before speaking.

"What was that about? Do you really think Roulain will give us Kira if we have historic proof that the diamond is gone?" Derrick asked, going over to the counter and grabbing a cookie.

"I don't think he would," Renee stated. "And even if George's dad finds out that the diamond is still down there, how are we going to find it? That station is huge, and we don't have much time."

Shannon shook her head. "No, the diamond doesn't matter anymore. And you're right, Roulain won't take any excuse for why we don't have it. This situation calls for drastic measures. That's why we had to get rid of Mr. van Gelder, because he'd never go for my plan." She walked over to the phone and picked up the receiver.

Derrick looked curious. "What plan is that?"

Shannon looked grave. "The one where we call Roulain up and tell him we have the diamond," she said. "Then we're going to set up a meeting with him, do a fake exchange, and save Kira."

Eight

THE EXCHANGE

"Are you *crazy*?" Renee shrieked. She started shaking her head. Derrick didn't look any more enthusiastic.

"You want us to do a fake exchange with Roulain?" he asked. "What makes you think he'll fall for it? What if he catches on?"

Shannon put the receiver back and sighed. "If we use a fake diamond, there's no way he'll know until he takes it to an appraiser or someone who'll tell him it isn't real. That should give us time to get Kira back." She looked directly at her fellow pyrates. "Face it, guys. The diamond's gone—there's no *way* we're going to find it down there. But Roulain still has Kira. When George's dad comes back, we're not going to be able to talk him out of going to the cops. And once the cops know, Roulain will know we don't have the diamond. Who knows what he'll do to Kira—and to us! We have to do something *now*."

George didn't know what to say. He'd had a feeling that Shannon's plan would be a little wacky, but trying to fool Roulain would be out-and-out dangerous. Would Roulain even agree to meet with the four of them? It seemed like he only wanted to conduct business through George's father. Surely he'd be a little suspicious when they showed up with a diamond in a baggie and no Mr. van Gelder in sight.

"I don't know, Shannon," he said finally, and Shannon sighed heavily. "I mean, this is really dangerous. If Roulain figures out we're trying to trick him, we'll all be in danger."

Shannon shook her head and ran a hand through her tangled, red-and-orange-streaked hair. "Not if we pull it off, George. It's all about acting. If we can convince him the diamond is real, we could have Kira back here before your father even gets home." She smiled hesitantly.

"I'm just not sure," George said, sitting down heavily in a kitchen chair. "It's a big risk. Maybe it wouldn't be so terrible for my dad to call the cops. They can't all be working for Roulain, right? And at least they know what they're doing . . . which is more than I can say for us."

Shannon frowned. "How can you *say* that, George? We knew enough to get as far as we have. And if your dad tells his whole story to a dirty cop, what do you think is going to happen to him?

Do you think anyone who's working for Roulain will protect us from the guy? No, it's more likely that your dad would just disappear quietly. He probably won't even make it home from the police station . . . because who's going to believe a crazy story like this, anyway?"

George's stomach clenched in fear. The thought of anything happening to his dad was terrifying. Now he regretted not having shared everything with his dad from the start. George had been scared that he wouldn't let him search for the diamond, but the treasure was the cause of all this trouble. Who cared about the diamond? George's priority now was keeping his dad safe. And finding Kira.

"You think the cops would hurt my dad?" he asked in a little voice.

"Not *the* cops," Shannon said quietly. "But *a* cop, if he happened to be on Roulain's payroll. And there's really no way for us to tell who is or isn't." She looked at her fellow pyrates. "Going to the cops isn't safe."

Derrick let out a huge sigh. "All right," he said finally. "Say we call Roulain and set up the exchange. What do we use for the diamond?"

Shannon smiled. "Actually, I have just the thing." She pulled a simple ring with a plastic gemstone off the ring finger of her right hand.

"I've been wearing it for luck ever since we started the treasure hunt." She held it up for all of them to see. George took it from her—the stone was about the size of a dime, and light enough that it was obviously fake.

"I'm not sure," he said. "It's awfully light. We'd have to weigh it down with something."

"That's easy enough," Renee murmured. "We could put it in a box with some coins in the bottom to make it heavier. And we could tell Roulain he can't hold it until he gives us Kira. If he picks it up, he'll be able to tell it's plastic right away."

"I think we can pull it off," Derrick said. "We wouldn't want him to grab the diamond without giving us Kira, especially if it was real. We can open the box and show it to him but not let him handle it." He glanced at George. "Sound good to you, George?"

George nodded slowly. There was something about all of this that wasn't sitting quite right, and he figured it was just that the whole thing was so dangerous. But it wasn't like they had a choice. They had less than an hour until his dad came back from the university archives—and as soon as he did, he'd call the police. And then who knew what might happen.

"All right," Shannon concluded, carefully prying back the metal prongs that held the gem in place. She shook the ring over her open palm, and the

huge plastic stone dropped out. Then she placed
the stone on the kitchen table. "We need to find a
little box to put this in, where we can tape some
quarters or nickels to the bottom of it and then
put some cotton or something in there."

"I'll get it," George offered, heading toward the
staircase.

"Not you," Shannon said quickly, grabbing the
back of his shirt and pulling him back. "Renee or
Derrick can go look for one. Right now I need
your voice."

George looked at Shannon in puzzlement.

"I'll go look," Derrick offered.

"Right. Um, I think my dad keeps some little
gift boxes in the first drawer of his dresser,"
George said. Then he turned his full attention to
Shannon. "Okay . . . you need my voice *why*?"

Shannon smiled. "Well, not your voice, actually.
More like your *dad's* voice."

"Ohhh," Renee murmured in comprehension.
George had a special talent for imitating voices.
He used to do it just for fun, but lately it had
come in handy pretty often.

George frowned. "You want me to imitate my *dad*?"

Shannon nodded encouragingly. "Just on the
phone. I don't think Roulain would agree to a
meeting if he knew that just us kids were involved.

He would know there was something weird going on if your dad had one of us call. So I think we should set up the meeting using your dad's voice, and then we can make up some excuse why he's not there when we get to the exchange spot."

George rocked on his feet. He *really* didn't like the sound of this. Sure, he had an uncanny knack for imitating people, but this was pushing things too far. They'd already tricked Roulain once. What if he suspected them of foul play? "Shannon, can't we give him a note or send him an e-mail?"

"Nope," Shannon responded in an instant. "We don't have time. We have to set up a meeting place within the hour." She picked up the phone and handed it to George.

"Oh, and make sure to choose a nice, public place," Shannon continued. "We want to make sure there are plenty of people around so Roulain can't just grab us or anything."

"Grab us. Right," he said, taking hold of the receiver. "Uh . . . what should I say, exactly?"

"It's all set," George said quickly, hanging up the phone. He let out a sigh of relief. He'd actually made it through the phone call without Roulain catching on! "Shorty's Diner. We'd better get going, guys. It'll take us a few minutes to walk over there."

Derrick, Shannon, and Renee all nodded solemnly. Renee pressed a tiny, gold-foiled box into George's hand. It felt heavy enough to contain the real diamond. George lifted the lid to see the plastic gem that Shannon had taken from her ring, then lifted up the cotton beneath to see a neat stack of three quarters taped directly in the center of the box's bottom. He smiled. "Good work, guys." Together the four of them headed for the front door.

"Wait a minute," George said when they were a few feet from the door. "If it's okay, I'd really like to leave from the basement window. I know it's silly, but we told my dad that we wouldn't go out the front door. Considering everything, I don't want to break our promise. It feels like it would be a bad omen."

Derrick nodded. "Sure thing, buddy," he said, turning back toward the basement steps.

Shannon and Renee followed. "No problem," Renee agreed. "At this point I think we can use all the help we can get."

It took about five minutes to get from George's basement to Shorty's Diner, which was just over three blocks away. Shorty's was a totally old-fashioned place. It had been on the same site for who knew how long. George and his dad had come here every weekend with George's mom. She had always ordered the blueberry waffles. George hadn't been there in years, but he suggested it as a meeting place to Roulain. He hoped that somehow, being in a place with so many good memories would bring them some good luck.

At lunchtime Shorty's was crowded with Wall Street employees, cramming into booths to enjoy a good, old-fashioned, greasy cheeseburger. But as George and his friends opened the front door, it was just before seven o'clock. It was almost dark. George knew that Shorty's closed at eight, and there weren't many people eating dinner now that the Wall Streeters had gone home. As George and his friends walked over to a big booth in the corner, they passed a college-aged couple, probably NYU students, eating burgers; three elderly men eating omelettes; and one lonely Wall Street type who was sipping coffee and kept checking his watch. Roulain wasn't there yet.

"I'm so nervous," Renee said as they slid into the booth. "I feel like a whole flock of butterflies are doing aerobics in my stomach."

"We just have to *believe* we can pull this off," Shannon said encouragingly. "If we act like we know what we're doing, Roulain will have no reason to be suspicious."

Just as she finished speaking, Shorty himself

walked over to their booth with an order pad. "You kids know what you want?" he asked.

"Oh, I don't think we—" George began, but Derrick cut him off.

"I'll take an extra-large cookies-and-cream milk shake with extra cookies," he said.

"All right," Shorty muttered, writing that down on his order pad. "Anyone else?"

George and his friends just shook their heads mutely. Satisfied, Shorty walked away.

"How can you *eat* at a time like this?" Renee demanded.

Derrick shrugged. "Hey, if this all goes sour and Roulain takes us hostage, at least I'll have had a really good milk shake."

Shannon seemed to consider this. "You know, that almost makes sense." She sat up and tried to get Shorty's attention. "Excuse me, Shor—"

But the bell on the door jangled and cut Shannon off. George looked over and sucked in his breath. There was Roulain—the same neighbor he had always known, dressed casually in a pair of black jeans and a New York Yankees sweatshirt. But now, for the first time, the sight of Mr. Roulain sent ice water running through his veins. Now George realized that Roulain wasn't the kind, understanding guy that George had always believed him to be.

That was just an act. Now George had to beat him at his own game.

Roulain was bad. He was scary. And he was going to do some horrible things to George and his friends if things didn't go their way.

Right behind Roulain were two of the goons that he'd employed in the tunnels. They were big and burly, and the one on the right had a long, crooked scar running from his nose to the corner of his mouth. Roulain quickly spotted George and his friends. As soon as Roulain headed toward the booth, George realized their mistake. George and his friends had all sat on the same side of the booth, with their backs to the kitchen. That meant to get away, they would have to run right by Roulain—which would make any kind of escape pretty impossible.

By the time Roulain arrived at the booth, an angry scowl had taken over his face. "Where's your dad?" he demanded furiously. "Peter van Gelder told me to meet him at this greasepit. He didn't say anything about you larvae being here."

"My dad is waiting outside," George forced himself to say. He was nervous and surprised by how normal his voice sounded. "If anything happens to us, he's going to come in here and clear things up. He wanted us to handle the exchange." George waited. That was the story Shannon had come up with on the way over. Would Roulain buy it?

Roulain frowned, first scanning the area outside the building, then looking from George, to Shannon, to Renee, to Derrick. Suddenly Shorty appeared behind him holding a massive milk shake with whipped cream and a cherry.

"Cookies-and-cream milk shake, extra cookies?" he asked.

"That's me," Derrick exclaimed happily. Shorty slid the milk shake across the table and placed the bill facedown.

"Enjoy!" he called, heading back to the kitchen.

Derrick grabbed the straw and took a big, greedy sip.

"All right," Roulain said finally, breaking the silence. He cast an annoyed eye at Derrick's milk shake, but he didn't say anything. "Let's get this over with."

"Where's Kira?" Renee asked, frowning at Roulain.

"She's in a safe place," Roulain replied. "You give me the diamond, I look at it, and then, if everyone keeps their promises, I take you to Kira and we exchange her for the diamond. I wasn't going to bring her to a place like this. What if she tried to get away?"

"Oh." Renee nodded, but her voice sounded uncertain. George guessed that they were all wondering the same thing: *Are we going to be able to fool Roulain long enough to get Kira back?*

"Okay," George said, summoning all his courage and lifting the small gold box, which was now damp from his sweaty hands, and placing it on the table. "Here's the diamond."

Roulain's eyes lit up. It was like saying, "Here's Santa Claus," to a little kid. Roulain looked at the box like he couldn't quite believe it was there. But there was something else in his eyes, too, something darker.

Hands shaking, George lifted the lid of the box and exposed the huge, plastic gemstone from Shannon's ring. It caught a beam of light from the old-fashioned lamp overhead and twinkled like it really was a priceless diamond. George could hear Roulain's breath catch. He reached out his hand to grab the stone, but before he got close, George snapped the box shut.

"I keep it," George insisted. "You can have the diamond after we get Kira and get out."

Roulain looked surprised for a second; then he began to chuckle. "Are you kidding?" he asked, shaking his head. "How am I supposed to check that it's the real thing?"

Shannon shrugged, trying to look confident. "You're going to have to trust us," she said. "Just like we're trusting you. It's only fair."

Roulain frowned, and his eyes shone as he turned to George. "But you *don't* really trust me, do you?" he asked. "I mean, you think I'll play straight because big bad Peter van Gelder is out there just waiting to put me in my place? That's why he didn't come in with you? Because he's playing watchdog?"

George felt a chill run down his spine. *He knows,* he realized suddenly. He could see it in Roulain's face and hear it in his voice. *Roulain knows that my dad's not out there. He knows we're all alone.*

Before George could even think about what that meant, Roulain reached out and grabbed the gold box out of his hands. "A-*ha!*" he shouted, ripping the box as he pulled it toward him and yanked off the top. "This is it, after five years of digging! My precious Eye of Eternity!" He reached in and grabbed the jewel, and immediately his face fell. George knew what that expression revealed: *It isn't real.* As soon as anyone handled the stone, they'd know it was plastic. "What—"

"*Run!!!*" Shannon screamed before Roulain could finish his sentence.

Nine

PYRATES IN MOTION

George flew out of the booth at Shorty's as if he were being shot out of a cannon. As soon as he was on his feet, he remembered their mistake. Roulain and his two goons were standing between them and the exit. There was only one way to go.

"The kitchen!" George cried.

Out of the corner of his eye he saw Derrick fling his cookies-and-cream milk shake in the direction of Roulain and his goons as he tore out of the booth. George opened the kitchen door and plowed through. He heard the milk-shake glass shatter and one of the goons shout, "Hey!" But George didn't turn around to see what was going on. He ran through the kitchen, around a huge sink, and past the startled short-order cook.

"Is there a back door?" George cried as he looked around. "It's an emergency!"

Wordlessly the stunned cook pointed to a nondescript door beside a gigantic refrigerator.

"Thanks!" George cried. He barreled toward it

and flung it open. Shannon was right on his heels, followed by Renee and Derrick. As George opened the back door, he could hear the kitchen door open again as Roulain and his goons stumbled through. It was now completely dark outside, and the yellowish light cast by the streetlamps reflected off the puddles in the back alley.

"There they are!" George heard one of the goons shout as he darted into the alley. "Get 'em!"

George ran as fast as he could down the alley, swerving around a huge, foul-smelling dumpster. As he ran, he could hear a skittering sound that he knew must be startled rats running back to shelter. Soon he had reached the end of the alley, a few feet from the intersection of Windsor Lane and William Street.

"We should split up," he gasped, panting. "We have a better shot that way. Just get back to my house any way you can."

"Okay, Captain," Shannon agreed.

Before anyone could say another word, George took off. He veered off down William Street and ran toward the next intersection. He didn't hear footsteps behind him, but he could still hear yelling in the vicinity of the diner. There were three bad guys and four in the pyrate crew. That meant three pyrates would be followed . . . and one would be free. Was he that one?

He paused at the intersection. *Don't turn back*, he told himself. *Just keep running*. But the question of whether anyone was on his trail was driving him crazy. He didn't hear anyone. Did that mean goons were following each of his friends? Were they all right?

He turned his head quickly.

It was enough. Behind him, still standing at the corner of William and Windsor, George could see the goon with the scar looking around, staring down each of the streets. In the millisecond it took George to glance around, he was spotted. Immediately the goon took off running up William Street after George. George froze for a second, then forced his feet to move and carry him away from Leroy's henchman.

"Give up, kid!" the goon yelled behind him. "I'm way bigger than you. You don't have a chance!"

"That's what you think," George whispered as he made a tight turn. His feet made squishy noises in the puddles as he bolted through an alley and came out on the other side. George wasn't sure anymore whether he was running toward or away from his house. The streets in downtown Manhattan were narrow and crowded, like a maze. In the darkness it was hard to tell one from another.

He was on a main street again, but he couldn't

tell which one. He had gained a few yards on the goon by ducking into the alley, but he could hear the man gaining on him. Quickly George turned right and continued running as fast as he could. A couple of blocks ahead, George could see the entrance to the Fulton Street subway station. The round green light that signaled the subway gave George an idea. Fulton Street was the nearest station to George's house, and he knew it pretty well. It was also a large station, with the A, C, J, M, Z, 2, 3, 4, and 5 trains all running through it. That meant that it sprawled under several city blocks—and had at least six or seven different entrances and exits.

It might be a good place to lose somebody.

George headed for the subway entrance with newfound conviction. He reached the staircase and headed down two at a time—*Please don't let me fall, please don't let me fall*. But when he was just about to reach the bottom of the stairs, he remembered one tiny detail: you had to *pay* to enter the rest of the subway station.

And George had left his MetroCard at home.

There was no time to buy a token. The entrance George had taken was small and nearly deserted except for one lonely, half-asleep-looking guy sitting in the token booth. As he flew off the staircase, George made a quick decision—he was going to have to jump over the turnstile and make a run for it.

He dashed toward the nearest gate, put his hands on the dividers on either side, and swung his legs over the metal turnstile.

"Hey!" the token-booth operator called, suddenly springing to life. "You can't sneak in there, kid! Security!"

George didn't have time to turn around. He dashed down the ramp to the A train, avoiding the commuters pushing on toward the exit. A few of them turned around to watch George, but not many. In the grand scheme of weird New York subway sights, an eleven-year-old boy jumping over a turnstile and running for his life probably didn't seem all that exciting.

Behind him George could hear the goon passing the token booth. "You stupid kid!" he yelled when he reached the turnstile. "You're not getting away that easily!" George heard, rather than saw, the goon land on the other side of the turnstile.

"*Hey!*" George heard the token-booth operator yell. "What the heck?!"

As fast as he could, George ran down the steps to the platform. It was hot down there—it always seemed warmer on the subway platforms than it was on the street above. About ten tired, bored-looking commuters were waiting for trains on either side of the platform. George dashed by them all, looking for the staircase that he knew led up to the 5 train.

As he reached the staircase on the other end of the platform and mounted the first step, he could hear the goon descending to the A platform. The goon's huge feet made a heavy *thunk thunk thunk* sound on the stairs. As George ran up the stairs to the 5 platform, he heard a huge *THUNK!* and then a cry of pain. This time George fought the urge to turn around. Had the goon actually fallen down the stairs?

George ran down the 5 platform and then up the staircase that led to Fulton Street. He couldn't help noticing that now he didn't hear any footsteps behind him.

Is it possible? George wondered. *Did I really lose that guy when he tripped?* He frowned. Fulton Street looked weirdly, perfectly normal. A few adults in business clothes walked past him into the station, and there were a couple of college students heading toward their dorm and some tourists looking around. It felt like just a normal, average weekday evening.

George's heart slowed down a bit. Maybe he was out of danger.

He figured it was best to get home as fast as he

could, though. *He* seemed to have lost his pursuer, but who knew what had happened to Shannon, Renee, and Derrick? Had they been as lucky? He started running again, this time back toward Windsor Lane.

What do we do now? The words kept echoing in George's head. *We couldn't find the diamond. We couldn't fake an exchange. What do we do now?*

George started to cross an intersection but then stepped back as he saw a delivery truck approaching. There was a stop sign at the intersection of Fulton and Windsor Lane, but few cars actually paid attention to it. George pondered the stop sign as he waited for the truck to pass. *We really need a stoplight here*, George thought. *Windsor Lane is pretty built up. It would be a lot safer. . . .*

Suddenly, as the truck pulled past him and he focused on the stop sign again, George's mind seemed to do a double take. An image of the four maps flashed before his eyes, all connected, forming a big circle of tunnels.

That's it! he thought, staring at the stop sign.

"Hey, kid!" A cabdriver who had actually stopped at the sign leaned out the driver's side window and yelled to George. "Hurry up and cross the street! I don't have all night!"

George looked at the cabbie. "Oh! Thanks! I

mean, sorry, sir!" He ran across the street, feeling like he was three feet from the ground. Suddenly things seemed possible again. Two blocks ahead he could see his house. As he approached, Derrick and Renee stuck their heads out from a nearby alley and ran toward the front stoop. *So they got away from the goons! All right! But what about Shannon?*

And . . . *uh-oh!* George's heart contracted in his chest.

Peter van Gelder was walking toward the house from the other direction.

George darted toward his front door, hoping that he could make it there before his father saw him, Derrick, and Renee. But he knew that was pretty much impossible. As he got closer to his front stoop, he could see his father spot him and frown in concern.

"*George?*" he heard his dad call out. "Is that *you*? What are you doing outside the house?"

By this time both George and his father had reached the front door, where Renee and Derrick were waiting. As George struggled for an answer, Shannon darted out of a deli across the street and ran over to meet up with the group.

"You made it!" Derrick greeted her. "So we're all safe. Excellent!"

Shannon looked at her friends, concerned. "I

was a little worried there for a while. I ended up
running through the Strand bookstore! I think I
lost him in paperbacks."

Peter van Gelder looked from George to his
friends, clearly not sure whether to ask for an explanation or ground George for life. "What's going on?
I thought I told you not to leave the house," he said
finally, fishing his house key out of his pocket and
stepping up to put it in the lock.

George shook his head. "It's a really long story,
Dad. And I'm really sorry we left. But I have
something more important to say—something you
all need to hear."

"More *important*?" Peter van Gelder didn't often
get mad, but he looked pretty upset right now.
"More important than disobeying me when all I
have in mind is your own safety? I couldn't be
more disappointed!"

"I know, Dad. I'm really sorry. The thing is . . ."
George paused as his dad turned the key in the
lock and pushed the door open.

"I think I know where the diamond is."

Ten

INTRUDER

"You *what*?"

Everyone turned and looked at George, but George didn't say anything. As soon as his dad had thrown open the front door, George could tell that something was wrong.

He stopped short.

"What is it, George? Where is the *diamond*?" Shannon urged. But George didn't answer her question.

Looking inside, George could see that the kitchen door was closed, but they hadn't left it that way.

"Shhh," he whispered. "Just a minute. I have a funny feeling here."

Everyone looked at George like he was nuts. But they all tiptoed into the house after him. As soon as they pushed open the door to the kitchen, it was clear that something was wrong.

They let out a collective yelp.

"Hey!"

"Oh, no!"

George's jaw dropped as he looked around the kitchen, his dad right behind him.

"Holy moley," his dad said.

The kitchen looked like a tornado had spun right through it. Someone had been there—looking for something. One of the chairs was overturned, and things were all out of place. The cabinets were open, and food was everywhere. There was an open jar of peanut butter on the counter, and the refrigerator door was wide open.

The group stood around, frozen in place.

It was really scary to think that someone else had been there. What if Roulain or one of his goons was in here? George walked across the room, stepping over food and silverware, to shut the refrigerator door.

He felt a cold chill climb up his spine as he looked around the kitchen. His heart pounded in his ears.

"Well, whoever did this, it looks like he didn't find what he was looking for and left," Derrick said.

"Do you think it was who I think it was?" Peter asked.

"Yes, probably. Roulain," Shannon stated blankly. "He sent his goons out to chase us, but he probably came back here himself. He must think we have the diamond and were trying to fool him so we could keep it."

"*Fool* him?" George's dad sounded pretty upset.

"We tried to fool him, Mr. van Gelder," Shannon admitted. "We wanted to get Kira back without calling the police. It was a really stupid idea—my idea. But we were getting—"

But then Shannon stopped.

No one spoke. They all listened.

"What was that noise?" Renee whispered, her face going white. "Do you have a cat, I hope?"

Mr. van Gelder, eyes wide, shook his head no.

Then another noise. Sort of a scrape, followed by a light bang.

This time *everyone* froze.

Silently George's dad reached down and picked up a saucepan that was lying on the floor. He motioned for the kids to stay where they were, and he began slowly, quietly walking toward the stairs.

George and his friends ignored his directions to stay and followed him to the foot of the stairs.

Mr. van Gelder began to climb the stairs one by one, avoiding all the squeaky places in the three-hundred-year-old steps. George did the same, turning around and pointing to the spots the rest of the group should avoid.

They got to the top of the second-floor steps and heard another noise.

It was coming from George's room! Somebody was *in* there! The door was almost closed, and they could hear the distinct sound of pages turning behind the door.

The journal, George thought. The idea of Roulain flipping through Kidd's book disgusted George. It didn't seem right.

They all gathered silently at the door, and Mr. van Gelder raised his saucepan. George started to count on his fingers: *One! Two! Three!* They threw open the door with a shout and dove in, prepared to do battle with Roulain himself. George was prepared to rip the journal right out of Roulain's hands.

But in the silence that greeted him, George opened his eyes wide and blinked.

The invader wasn't Roulain at all.

It was *Paul*!

He was sitting on George's bed with a pint of Ben & Jerry's Mint Chocolate Cookie ice cream in one hand and a spoon in the other. And he had a bunch of George's comic books spread out in front of him.

George was so relieved, he laughed out loud, and the rest of the group soon joined him. Paul just looked at the five of them, stunned. He clearly thought they'd all gone a little crazy.

"What are you doing here, Paul?" Shannon said, wiping tears of laughter from her eyes. Paul had closed the curtains in George's room so that almost no light crept in. He had been sitting in the dark.

Now he was shielding his eyes from even the dim light coming in from the hall.

"Hi," Paul said. He dipped his spoon into the half-melted ice cream and took a sloppy bite. "I overheard something in the tunnels. I know you were worried about your friend, so I came up here to tell you guys. You weren't here, so I decided to wait for you. And then I realized how hungry I was and I got food. I'm sorry for just coming in, but—"

"I'm glad it's you!" George said. *And so relieved you're not Roulain,* he thought. "You can come here for food anytime you want." Paul gave a tiny hint of a smile; there was a ring of ice cream around his mouth. George thought that a person must not get a lot of practice eating ice cream or cleaning up after himself in the kitchen if he lived underground.

"How did you get in the house?" Shannon asked.

"Easy," Paul said, shrugging. "I just walked to the part of the tunnel that's under your basement, and the rope was just dangling there, so I grabbed onto it and climbed up."

"With your bare hands?" Renee asked. "All by yourself?" Paul nodded. "Wow. "

Paul looked down with some embarrassment at the container of ice cream. "I'm sorry I ate almost all of it. I was really hungry," he said.

"It's no problem, Paul," George said. "So you like Ben and Jerry's?"

"Who?" Paul asked with a frown of confusion.

"The ice cream," George said, starting to laugh again. "It's called Ben and Jerry's."

"It was good." Paul smiled back. "Really, really good. Almost as good as Oreos." Paul dug his spoon in again and shoveled out another gigantic bite, which he stuffed into his mouth. A few melted drops fell off the spoon and landed on George's comforter. George didn't care. He was just happy to see Paul like this, aboveground, eating ice cream like a normal kid—well, almost.

Shannon sat down on the bed beside Paul. Ever since Shannon had brought Paul the two bags of Oreos that she'd promised him, it had seemed like Paul was closest to her. George felt pretty close to Paul, too. About a week ago, when the others had temporarily given up on their pyrate quest, George and Paul had explored part of the tunnels together. When they had been stranded on an underground lake, they had shared stories of their mothers and had realized that they actually had a lot in common.

"So how does it feel to be on the dayside?" Shannon asked Paul.

"Um. Fine. It was pretty bright before, though," he said through a mouthful of ice cream. "It's not so bad at night if there aren't any brights."

"What made you do it?" Derrick asked. "I thought you *never* wanted to come up to the dayside."

Everybody pushed in a little closer to hear his answer. George knew that Paul was petrified of being aboveground.

"Well," Paul began, "I was spying on Roulain's goons, and I heard them say some stuff that I thought you might wanna know."

"Really? What was it?" George's dad broke in. He was anxious to know about anything that might help them find Kira. His excitement made Paul shrink back a little.

"It's okay, Paul," Shannon assured him, putting a hand on his arm. "We're happy you came to tell us. What did you hear?"

"Well, the goons were back guarding the elevator to Roulain's apartment. First they talked about how you ran away from them at a diner—they were really mad about that—and then they said they were in charge of moving a woman to a boat, but they didn't say who or where." He looked around. "Does that help you?"

"I bet the woman they're moving is Kira." George's dad sighed heavily. "Unfortunately, there is more than one marina in Manhattan. We have no idea which one they'd be at. We *could* check them all, but it would take time. . . ."

They all sat in silence. And then suddenly Derrick let out a whoop.

"Wait a second, guys! Check this out!" He unzipped one of his jacket pockets and reached his hand inside. He pulled out a small leather case, about the size of a large calculator. "Ta da! Remember this? The handheld computer I found back in the tunnel! It's just an address book—full of a bunch of random names and numbers, and I thought it was totally useless. But maybe . . ." Derrick pressed the tiny button on its side to turn it on. *"R-o-u-l-a-i-n,"* Derrick said out loud as he typed in the password.

Derrick used the arrow keys to click on the address book, and everyone gathered around it to see.

"Look!" Derrick cried. "Here's an entry for the St. Johns." He clicked on it with the tiny pointer that came with the computer, and the St. Johns' entry came up.

"There's a note here," Derrick said. "Eight DVD players, two VCRs, five televisions, Model 15A." He looked up at George. "That must be their most recent order. The TVs have a check mark next to them—maybe that's what Roulain had in stock, and they had to steal the rest."

George's dad nodded solemnly. "That sounds possible, Derrick. When this is all over, the police may like to have this as evidence." He sighed. "Now, as for the boat—maybe we should look under *M*, for 'marina'?"

Derrick nodded and scrolled down. "I don't see anything, Mr. van Gelder."

"Hmmm." George's dad frowned. "Maybe Y, for 'yacht club'?"

Derrick continued scrolling and shook his head. "Nothing. Any other ideas?"

Shannon leaned over the computer's screen and then furrowed her brow. "What about B?" she asked. "For 'boat'?"

Derrick nodded and started scrolling up.

"Aha!" George's dad said. "You were right, Shannon! Look, it says right there, 'L.'s boat—Battery Park marina, #4C29.' I bet that's where they've taken the woman. It has to be Kira!" Peter cried with a big grin. "Don't you think, kids?"

"It sure sounds like it," Renee agreed.

"Now we know where Kira is," Derrick piped in. "If we only had the diamond."

"Wait! That's just what I was saying when we came in the door," George said excitedly. "I got distracted by the mess and thinking somebody had broken into the house. But I think I figured out where the diamond is!"

"Really?" Renee said in disbelief. "Are you kidding?"

"Nope, I'm completely serious. Follow me and I'll show you." George ran down the stairs with his father and most of the rest of the gang close behind.

Only Paul stayed behind, wanting to avoid the "brights" and finish up his ice cream. George led his dad and his friends to the kitchen, where the maps were laid out on the kitchen table.

"Look at the exits," George insisted.

"Yeah, they're in a circle—we already know that," Shannon said impatiently.

"It's not necessarily a circle. Look, it could also be an *octagon*!" George insisted. "The handle on the trapdoor is an octagon! And it's about forty feet away from the mast."

Shannon jumped out of her seat. "It's forty feet *straight up*!"

"Of course!" Derrick exclaimed, standing up. "George, you're brilliant."

"Okay, can you go over that once more?" Peter asked.

Derrick leaned over and traced the shape with his finger. "The shape of this pattern matches the shape of the handle on the trapdoor. And the trapdoor is forty feet away from the mast right underneath it!"

"Oh! And look back at the third clue! *'To seize thy fate, connect the pieces of eight'*!" Renee said excitedly. "Maybe Captain Kidd was telling us to connect the eight exits!"

"So are you saying the diamond is in the doorknob?" Peter van Gelder asked.

"That's right, Dad. It has to be."

"Well, what are we waiting for?" Renee said, already halfway to the basement stairs.

Shannon knocked over her chair as she rushed to get up but left it that way. They were in a hurry, and the kitchen was still so messy that it didn't make any difference.

They had a *diamond* to claim!

Everyone flew down the stairs.

It was dim down there in the light of the hanging bulb, and the group was hushed as they gathered around the trapdoor. Now that they'd deciphered the clues, the knob seemed to gleam with a light from within. George wondered whether he was imagining things.

Was there really a diamond inside?

They all knew that if the diamond *wasn't* in there, this was the end of the road. They had really run out of ideas. But if it *was,* then this was just the beginning. Then they would have to embark on a new adventure: trying to rescue Kira.

Mr. van Gelder stood up, walked over to his tool chest that sat on a nearby shelf, and pulled out a hammer. "George, I think you should do the honors." He handed it over.

George took the hammer and got down on his knees in front of the door. *Here goes,* he thought as he raised the hammer over his head. *This is what our whole adventure comes down to.*

"Wait!" said Shannon. "What if you break the diamond when you hit the doorknob?"

"There's no way," Derrick said. "A diamond is the hardest natural substance on earth. Don't you pay attention in science class?"

"Oh, yeah, that's right. I forgot." Shannon laughed nervously.

Once again, with a big flourish, George lifted the hammer up a few feet, then brought it down on the doorknob.

SMASH!

The glass handle crumbled into a million pieces. At first it was hard to tell if the diamond was even there because the knob was now just a pile of sparkly, broken glass. Everyone leaned in to take a closer look.

"Where is it?" Shannon asked in an eager voice. "Does anyone see the diamond?"

George stuck his hand down in his sleeve to brush away the glass . . . and they all gasped. There it was. The biggest diamond any of them had ever seen, right there. On his basement floor.

George picked it up and held it in the palm of his hand. For a few seconds they all just stared at it.

Derrick finally broke the silence.

"Wow," he said in a hushed whisper. "The Eye of Eternity!"

Eleven

OPERATION: SAVE KIRA

The diamond glittered brightly, even in the dark basement. It was roughly the size of a marble. It reflected back brilliant shades of blue, white, and green all at once.

"Can I hold it?" Derrick asked reverently.

George nodded, and Derrick lifted it gently out of George's palm.

"It's so heavy," Derrick said with awe. "We're rich. I know we have to give it to Roulain, but until we do . . . just for this little while, we're incredibly rich."

"We've found Captain Kidd's treasure," George whispered. "I knew we would. I knew we were *meant* to." He sighed. He'd always felt connected to Kidd, but right now—at this very moment—he could almost feel Kidd's pride and relief.

George took the diamond back into his hand and they all sat quietly in the dim light, watching it sparkle. George thought of all the years it had been hidden—all the years it had been a mystery.

He looked at his dad, who smiled at him. George could see the admiration shining in his dad's eyes. It was a nice feeling. George knew his dad must be eager to get the diamond to Roulain save Kira, but he seemed to understand that George and his friends needed a few quiet minutes to enjoy their triumph.

"We did it, you guys," Shannon said.

"George, I said it once and I'll say it again: You're brilliant," Derrick said. "How you figured out the octagon clue, I'll never know. It's almost like you have a sixth sense about this stuff."

"It wasn't a sixth sense," George said, smiling. "It was a stop sign."

"Huh?" Derrick looked confused.

"I saw a stop sign when I was running from the goons," George explained. "I just looked at it and something clicked in my head and—"

"Right," Derrick said. "Whatever. Like I said, you're brilliant."

"Hey, you guys," Renee broke in, "let's have three cheers for our captain before we go!"

"Good idea," Peter van Gelder said. "To Captain George!"

George's friends joined in with his dad. They gave George three full rounds of hip hip hoorays and clapped.

With everyone smiling at him, George couldn't help feeling embarrassed, but he also couldn't deny that he felt proud.

"Let's take it upstairs and show Paul," Shannon said. "We couldn't have done this without him."

They all hurried back up the two flights of stairs to George's room. George cradled the diamond carefully in his hands. He had never held anything so valuable before, and it was the most amazing feeling in the world.

Shannon knocked on the door to George's room. "Paul," she called, "we have a surprise for you."

"Oreos?" he asked in an excited voice.

She pushed open the door. "No, but we *do* have the treasure."

Paul's mouth dropped open and he watched, amazed, as the five of them stepped into the room. George held out the diamond for Paul to see.

He seemed to want to say something, but no sound came out.

"Wow . . ." he said finally. "Where was it?"

"It was in my house all along," George told him. "It was in the doorknob on the trapdoor. Here, you can hold it for a minute." He held it out and Paul took it.

"So this is a diamond," Paul murmured. "My mom told me it was like a clear rock, but I've never seen anything like this before. It hurts my eyes, it's so pretty."

George smiled. *My mom would love to see this diamond,* he thought. *She would have loved to have been here for this whole adventure. She would have loved every minute.* But somehow, even though George wished his mother could have been alive to see this happen, he felt certain that she was with him—that her old pirate stories had helped him survive the tunnels, that her own fascination with Kidd had helped him believe it was possible to find the treasure. *Thank you, Mom,* he thought.

"We wouldn't have found it without your help, you know," Shannon told Paul. "We really owe you."

"Oh . . . well . . ." Paul looked away. He probably wasn't used to people thanking him, George realized.

"Listen," George's dad said, "I hate to interrupt, but we should think about Kira. I want to go and get her now before anything bad happens."

"Of course. You're right," Shannon said. "Let's get going. Should we just go straight to the marina and try to find the boat?"

George's dad's face turned stern. "No, kids. We are not going anywhere. Your parents would never forgive me if anything happened to you. I'm going alone," he stated in a voice that George recognized. It was his "I'm not going to change my mind" voice. "I said I wouldn't put you in any more danger, and I meant it. I have to do this myself. You've all been amazing, but I can't let you get close to Roulain again. It's too dangerous."

Renee was the first to object. "I'm sorry, Mr. van Gelder, but we do everything together, and we have to see this thing through to the end. Our parents would understand if they knew how important this is. You can't ask us to stay behind now!"

Peter van Gelder sighed. "But I'm telling you to. You kids are not coming with me, and that's that. In fact, I think you should all go home where you'll be safe. George will let you know when I get back with Kira."

"But Mr. van Geld—" Derrick began to speak, but George's dad cut him off.

"Derrick, you've all been through enough."

No one else spoke, but they glanced around at each other, communicating with their eyes. They all knew that they certainly weren't heading home now—in fact, they would go to the marina anyway, as soon as George's dad was out of the house. He might need them.

"I want each of you to promise me that once I leave this house, you will *not* follow me. I really mean it this time."

George looked around and saw Derrick, Renee, and Shannon wearing expressions of disappointment.

He looked at Paul. Paul caught his eye and pointed down to the ground. *Of course,* George thought. *The tunnels!*

"I promise," George said. "We won't follow you. Right, guys?" George gave everyone a meaningful look.

"I promise, too," Derrick said.

"Yeah, me too," Shannon agreed.

"O-okay," Renee said reluctantly.

"I know it seems like I'm being harsh," George's dad said with a sigh as he left. "But I couldn't live with myself if anything happened to you."

"It's all right," Shannon said.

"Now, kids, I'm going to have to take the diamond with me," his dad went on.

"Wait!" Derrick interrupted. "Just let me hold it again for one more second before I'm broke again, like I was this morning." He took the gem from George, gave it a little kiss good-bye, and then handed it to George's dad. George's dad put it in the breast pocket of his fleece pullover and then zipped the zipper, patting the pocket afterward to feel the stone inside.

"Let's head downstairs."

"Maybe you should take one of the walkie-talkies with you, just in case," Shannon suggested. "That way if you get into trouble, you can call for help."

"Good idea," George said. "Also, you could wear it on your belt and leave it turned on so we can hear what's happening. That way we'll know if you need help or if you want us to call the police." That idea made George feel much better. If they could hear what was happening, they could be sure to catch up with him if something went wrong.

"I suppose I could do that," Mr. van Gelder said. "That sounds like a pretty good idea, actually."

They gave him a walkie-talkie, and he clipped it to his belt and turned the dial to "transmit" mode.

The rest of the group tuned their walkie-talkies in to his signal.

"Okay, then. I think I'm as ready as I'll ever be," George's dad said. He took a deep breath. "Wish me luck, kids. I'm off to rescue Kira."

George looked at his dad and felt a little scared. What if something *did* happen to his father as he tried to exchange the diamond for Kira? George didn't completely trust Roulain. But they'd come this far: The only way to get Kira back was to give Roulain the diamond and hope for the best. Besides, George knew that he and his friends would be right behind his dad, ready to help. George stepped forward and gave his father a quick hug. "Dad, we'll be listening closely. Just give us the signal if you want us to call the cops."

"What should the signal be?" George's dad asked.

George smiled. "How about, 'Kids, call the cops'?"

"Okay," Peter van Gelder agreed with a laugh. "I guess that'll work just fine. All right, then, I'm off."

"Good luck," Derrick, Renee, and Shannon chorused.

"Good luck, Dad."

George watched his father walk out the front door and couldn't help but be concerned. At the same time last week George had believed his dad was no more than a tea-sipping historian. But now he was going off to confront a group of dangerous thugs! George knew his dad was smart, but he wasn't sure Peter van Gelder would know how to deal with Roulain. He was far from the secret-agent type.

Everyone listened quietly to the walkie-talkies to be sure that they were working.

"Okay, George," Renee said skeptically. "I know from that look you gave us that we're not just going to stay here. But you heard your dad. We're not supposed to follow him."

"Yeah," Shannon said. "What's your plan, George?"

"It's not *my* plan," George said, turning to Paul. "It's his." George looked at Paul, who gave a little smile. He actually looked proud.

"What is it, Paul?" Derrick asked. "You know a

way that we can follow George's dad without *following George's dad?*"

"We'll go through the tunnels," Paul said, sounding more confident than George had ever heard him sound before. "I know an exit that lets out only a few feet away from the marina."

"Ha! That's great!" Derrick almost shouted. "If we take the tunnels, then we're not technically following him. We're taking a totally different route to the same place!"

"And there are no streets to cross or cars to watch out for. We might even get there before your dad does, George," Shannon said excitedly.

"All right, gang, let's go!" George started heading downstairs.

A part of George felt bad about deceiving his father again. Obviously his dad hadn't meant that they could go with him as long as they took a different route. But George was worried about his father going up against Roulain. Roulain could be ruthless and irrational.

"Are you all ready?" asked George. Everyone nodded. "Good!" he said. "Let's get down to the basement and get moving. Operation: Save Kira is ready to start!"

Twelve

THE FIFTH PYRATE

One by one, each of them slipped down the rope that led from George's basement to the tunnels. They went faster than they ever had before. At the bottom of the shaft the pyrates unclipped their harnesses, turned on their helmet lights, and looked at Paul. George noticed that Paul didn't even complain about the "brights" anymore. *Maybe his eyes are just adjusting,* George thought. *Or maybe he has more important things on his mind.*

"All right. First we need to go to the abandoned subway station," Paul said, and headed off in that direction without waiting for a reply. George and his friends nodded at each other and then followed Paul.

The farther George went, the more static he heard from his walkie-talkie. He could hear the same muffled buzz from the walkie-talkies clipped to his friends' belts. He caught Renee's eye, and Renee must have seen his concern.

"The walkie-talkies can only transmit over a certain

distance," Renee said. "Now that we're forty feet underground, we're too far from your dad to pick up his signal. I'm sure he'll come back when we're above-ground again. There's no way he's made it to the marina yet."

George nodded. "I hope not," he said. "It just makes me nervous. Let's hurry up and get there!"

Still moving quickly, the pyrates walked down the tunnel and clambered up a rock pile that led to a different tunnel. Silently they expertly squeezed through the narrow part, finally following Paul into the wide, empty, abandoned subway station.

"This way," Paul whispered. They walked in the same direction they had headed weeks ago, when they'd come across a room full of pirate things and an open room that was filled with stray cats. But they took an early turn and headed into a narrow tunnel with a steep incline. George could feel his chest heaving as he struggled to keep up. The rocky uphill terrain made the climb hard work!

"Are we close, Paul?" George whispered.

"Almost there," Paul promised without turning around.

"It's a good thing you showed up, Paul," Renee said as they struggled along. "First you tell us where Kira is, and then you find an alternate route. We're lucky to have you as part of the group."

"I'm part of the group?" Paul didn't turn around, but his voice sounded funny.

"Of course you are," Derrick said.

"You've been with us from the beginning," Shannon said. "And we would never have found half the clues or known our way around down here without you."

George broke in, "Plus, you saved me from Roulain's goon that time."

"Well, you saved me from the goons, too," Paul replied.

George considered his friends' words. It was true: Paul had helped them out so much that they could never thank him enough. And it somehow seemed like he was always tagging along with them—that he was never an "official" member of their pyrate crew.

"Hey, I have an idea," George said. "When we have a chance, don't you think Paul should really join the pyrate crew?"

"The pyrate crew?" Paul asked, confused.

"You mean like have him take the oath?" asked Derrick. "Definitely! I don't know why we didn't think of it sooner."

"Absolutely," Shannon agreed. "Paul's definitely earned it. He's one of us!"

"I agree," Renee said. "Let's do it!"

Paul turned around, his face all lit up. "Really? I'll really be a part of the group?"

"Yes!" Shannon said excitedly. "Once we get to the marina, we can do the oath there."

Suddenly there was a hissing sound, then some static, and then there was a voice. It was like George's dad was right there in the tunnel with them. ". . . this the Battery Park marina, on the left?" they heard his voice ask.

Then another voice broke in, a stranger's: "Yeah, just go in that blue door and talk to the receptionist. She'll help you out."

"Thanks," Peter van Gelder's voice replied.

George and his friends smiled at each other. Hearing his dad's voice made George feel a million times better. He was still safe!

"We must almost be there," Derrick said.

"That's right," said Paul. "The exit is right around this corner."

They all followed Paul around a narrow turn, and sure enough, they were facing a grate with a muted streetlight shining through!

"All *right*!" Shannon cried with a huge smile.

"And just in the nick of time, too," Renee added. "George's dad is probably in the office now."

Confidently Paul pushed a latch on the grate and it popped open. The pyrates stepped out hesitantly.

They were in a small area enclosed by boulders. It was completely dark now—George wasn't sure, since his watch had broken about a week ago, but he thought it must be around nine o'clock. He could hear the swishy sounds of the Hudson River to their left, and there was grass underfoot.

"We're in Battery Park," Derrick said, looking around. "Let's head for the marina, guys!"

"Where *is* the marina?" Shannon asked, looking in all directions.

"This way," George explained. He had been to the marina once before, a couple of years ago, to take a Sunday afternoon ride on the St. Johns' speedboat. Mr. St. John had talked a lot about how expensive it was to keep a boat in the city and said he might sell it. *Good thing they had it then,* George thought as he and his friends ran over. *At least I got to know where the marina was!*

When they were within a few yards of the marina office, they stopped and listened. They could hear George's dad talking to the receptionist. They heard him explain that he was there to meet up with a friend and that he couldn't remember which boat was his.

"That blue-and-white speedboat with the flag— is that Jean Roulain's?" Mr. van Gelder asked.

Then they heard an unfamiliar voice say, "No, but

close. It's the silver powerboat. You see it—way out there today, isn't it? *That's* Roulain's. Saw him go out there in the dinghy a couple of hours ago, but he hasn't moved his boat at all. Must just be relaxing out there. Most folks come in after sunset, but I'll bet he's enjoying the city view."

"Perfect night for it," they heard George's dad reply, "Thanks a million."

"Are you going out to his boat?" the receptionist asked. "Let me radio him and tell him you're on your way. He'll probably want to come get you in the dinghy."

"Um, no, don't call him," they heard Mr. van Gelder say quickly. "It's his birthday, and I want to surprise him."

Good save, Dad! George thought.

"Hmmm, his birthday," the other voice said, sounding a bit doubtful. "Are you sure? I guess I could get one of the attendants to bring you out in the powerboat."

"Oh, that would be perfect," George's dad agreed.

"I wouldn't want to ruin the surprise," the attendant went on. "I love surprises myself, you know. Why, just last week my granddaughter . . ." They heard a door open and shut.

After a few minutes they could hear the loud whir of the powerboat motor. And then George's dad said,

"Thanks a lot, but I'm just going to jump out into this dinghy here. You know. For the surprise and all."

"All right, suit yourself," they heard an unfamiliar voice say.

"There he goes," Shannon said when they heard a splash. They were hanging back behind the last corner, waiting for him to hit the water.

"Let's just stay here for a few more minutes while he gets a little ways out," George said.

They could hear his dad grunting as he worked hard to row against the current of the Hudson River.

When they finally went down to the edge of the water, George's dad was far enough away that there was no way he could see them.

"Should we just sit down here to wait and listen?" Derrick asked.

"I guess so. I don't know what else we can do," Renee said.

They all sat down on the grass by the river. It was really dark, and the city lights reflected in the water twinkled.

Paul had his arms crossed in front of his chest, but he was looking at the lights and the water in amazement.

"I've never seen anything like this," he said. "It's so beautiful. Look at the buildings!"

Shannon smiled. "It really is. Aren't you glad you came up to see it?"

Paul nodded. "Definitely. It's different than I thought."

"Seems to me that now would be a good time to do the new improved pyrate oath with Paul," Shannon said.

"Great idea!" Renee agreed.

The pyrate oath was the vow that they had taken with each other at the beginning of their adventure. It was a set of promises that they had made to each other based on an oath listed at the back of Captain Kidd's journal. The deal was sealed by spitting in your hand and then stacking it with the group.

Derrick called this a "spit sandwich." Actually, George couldn't believe he was going to go through another one. It was pretty gross.

But when he saw the look on Paul's face, he knew it was going to be worth it.

Paul was practically beaming as he looked around at his group of friends. His eyes shone in the night.

"You remember it, right, Derrick?" George asked. "I forgot to bring the journal."

"Of course," said Derrick. "Have I ever failed you?"

They all got in a circle and held hands. Derrick solemnly recited the oaths out loud, asking Paul if he promised to abide by each one.

"Paul, do you swear to be true and loyal to your captain?"

"Who's my captain?" he asked. "George?"

They nodded.

"Yes, I promise," he said seriously. George shot him a little smile.

Derrick went on. "Do you promise never to steal from those who don't deserve it?"

Paul didn't hesitate. "Yes, I promise."

"Do you promise to always share spoils justly?" he asked.

"Spoils?" He looked at Derrick, confused.

"That's the treasure we collect," Renee whispered.

"Oh, okay. And 'justly'? What's that?"

"Fairly," Renee told him.

"Okay. Yes, I promise to share . . . spoils . . . justly."

"And finally, never harm innocents. Do you promise never to harm innocents?"

"Yes," Paul said, "I promise."

"All right," Derrick said. "Way to go, Paul. Now we've come to my least-favorite part."

George laughed as Shannon leaned forward. "Right, now what you do is you spit into your hand like this," she said. She spit a big, messy glob into her hand. George, Derrick, and Renee did the same.

Paul looked at them like they were all crazy. But then he spit in his hand, too.

"Now everybody puts their hands together in the middle like this, one on top of the other."

Ewww, George thought. He cringed as he put his hand in.

"Welcome, Paul," he said.

"Welcome, Paul," everyone echoed.

"I'm very happy to be a part of your group," Paul said in a formal tone.

"I'm glad you're happy, Paul," Shannon said.

Just then there was a crackle on the walkie-talkies. They all looked over at the river and saw that George's dad had made it all the way to the boat and was climbing over the railing onto the deck.

"Hey!" His yell was transmitted over the walkie-talkie. "Kira! Roulain! Are you here?"

George and the rest of the crew stood up and ran to the water, straining to see the boat.

"I have binoculars," Renee told them as she unzipped her backpack.

But another boat had drifted in front of Roulain's boat, blocking their view.

The radio crackled again, and suddenly they heard Roulain's voice: "Van Gelder! You're pretty brave to show up after that stunt your brat pulled earlier. You'd better have the diamond!"

George could hear his dad panting from the effort of rowing out there and climbing on board. "I've got the diamond, and I know that Kira is here," he said in a steely voice. "I want to make the exchange."

"Oh, really?" Roulain asked, like he was making fun of George's dad. "You and those kids finally pulled it together, huh? Well, you're lucky I'm going to give you another chance. Let's see the diamond."

"Not until I see Kira," George's dad insisted.

There was a pause, and then they heard somebody sigh. "All right," Roulain's voice agreed. Hinges creaked as a door was opened. "This way. In here. There she is."

There was a gasp of relief, and then they heard Kira's voice! "Oh, Peter! Are you all right? Why are you here?"

George and his friends all gave each other relieved looks. *Kira's okay!*

"Are you hurt, Kira?" George's dad asked in a worried tone. "Did he hurt you?"

"I'm fine. I'm not hurt," she replied. "I'm so relieved to see you."

"That's enough mushy stuff, you two," Roulain's harsh voice broke in. "I showed you Kira. Now you show me the diamond."

There were some muffled sounds. George guessed his dad was unzipping his jacket and retrieving the diamond. "Here it is," Peter van Gelder said.

There was a pause as Roulain took in the Eye

of Eternity. "Hand it over, van Gelder!" he practically shouted after a moment.

"No," George's dad said. "First you untie Kira and let her get in the dinghy. I don't want you going back on your word."

"First give me the diamond, and then I'll untie her!" Roulain sounded furious now.

"No deal, Roulain."

"I said, give me the diamond!"

George and the group gasped collectively as they heard the start of a scuffle on the radio. George's dad shouted, "*Hey!* That's not the deal!"

"Tough luck!" Roulain shouted. "It's mine now! You're too slow, van Gelder!"

George let out a moan. "I think Roulain got ahold of the diamond and he still has Kira!" This was just the situation George had feared.

But then . . . *Thwump! Thwump!* It sounded like punches were being thrown, and Roulain shouted, "Give it back to me, van Gelder, or your girlfriend gets it!"

"You'll have to kill me first, Roulain!" George's dad shouted. "But not before I throw this diamond into the Hudson!"

"*No!*" they heard Kira yell. "Peter! Please don't throw away the Eye of Eternity! It's priceless to my people!"

"Fine, van Gelder!" Roulain shouted. "If you won't hand it over, then you're coming with me. I'll get the diamond sooner or later, and that'll be the end of both of you!"

Just then a gust of wind came up and moved the boat that had been blocking their view. Renee immediately raised the binoculars. The walkie-talkie got a blast of static and then stopped transmitting Peter's signal.

"Oh, *no*! Roulain is out on deck, pulling up the anchor!" Renee cried. "And I think the signal just went out!"

George jumped up and strained to look. "Do you think he's just bluffing, or is he really going to take off with my dad on board?"

"He's starting the engine—I can see smoke coming out of the back."

"I can't believe this," George said, panicking, "He's got my dad and Kira *and* the diamond. What are we going to do? We can't even hear them anymore."

There was silence for a minute. George watched as the boat that held his father began to drift away. He had a sinking feeling in the middle of his chest—*Not my dad! I was just starting to figure out how cool he is, and now he's being taken away!*

"Wait!" he cried. "The St. Johns used to have a

boat. They may have sold it, but if they haven't—they can get us out there!"

Everyone's face brightened. Renee nodded eagerly.

"She said we should ask her if we needed help of any kind. I think we need some help here. We have no idea what's happening on board," Renee said, her voice rising in fear.

"You're right," George said. "I'll call the St. Johns."

Shannon dug in her backpack for her tiny cell phone and handed it to George, who punched in the St. Johns' number and prayed that someone would pick up.

Thirteen
JOLLY ROGER

Mr. and Mrs. St. John arrived at the marina almost immediately, their faces flushed with concern and confusion. George felt kind of sorry for them. He knew his call must have alarmed them.

"What's going on here? Where is your father, George?" Mr. St. John asked right away, before George could greet them.

"It's a really long story, but the short version is that Kira and my dad are on Roulain's boat and he's kidnapped them both. Roulain just pulled up anchor and took off. We need a boat to go after them."

At the mention of Roulain's name, Mrs. St. John's eyes went steely. "I knew things were more serious than Peter would admit. Roulain is trouble. Let's go."

George felt relief wash over him. "You still have your boat?"

"Yes, indeed," Mr. St. John put in. "We will go after him, but I want to hear the whole story. I want to know what we're getting into."

"Sure—we'll tell you on the way," George said.

The whole lot of them ran toward the docks: Mr. and Mrs. St. John, George, Renee, Derrick, Shannon, and Paul. They located the St. Johns' boat, a red-and-white speedboat, and Mr. and Mrs. St. John worked as a team to get it unmoored. As George climbed in, he noticed that Paul was still standing on the dock, looking uncomfortable, shuffling from one foot to the other.

George smacked himself on the forehead. "Oh, *Paul*! I'm sorry." George knew that Paul had a fear of water. They had taken a raft across the underground lake because they were trapped, and Paul had nervously held the raft handles the whole way.

Paul frowned, looking out over the river. "I've never been on big water this big," he murmured.

George reached out to take Paul's hand. "Paul, it's okay. I'll help you in. This is a much bigger boat than the raft we were on before. It's much safer, and you're with all of us."

Shannon turned around. "Paul, it's okay. It's safe, I promise."

With George's help, Paul slowly climbed on. He tentatively stepped on the boat's floor and looked all around. Then Mrs. St. John seemed to notice Paul for the first time. "Now, wait a minute. . . . I don't think I've met this gentleman."

Shannon introduced them. "Mrs. St. John, this is our friend Paul. He was like our guide in the tunnels. He actually grew up underground. This is the first time he's been on the dayside in a long time."

Mrs. St. John nodded. Since she had been in the tunnels, George guessed she must have heard the term "dayside" before. "Well, it's very nice to meet you, Paul."

"Ummm . . . yes," Paul said, and quickly looked away. It seemed to George that he had no idea how to react when people were nice to him. He still looked pretty nervous about being on the water until Mrs. St. John walked over and gave him a warm smile.

"If it's your first time on a boat, it might be best to sit down," she said gently. "I'll sit right next to you. It doesn't take long to get used to being on a boat. So, what are your impressions of the dayside so far?"

Shannon shot Mrs. St. John a grateful smile. "He really likes ice cream. Ben and Jerry's especially."

"Ice cream, huh?" Mrs. St. John grinned at Paul. "Well, Paul, let me tell you about the time Mr. St. John and I actually toured the Ben and Jerry's factory up in Vermont and . . ."

George flashed Shannon the thumbs-up sign and sat down facing the river. *We're coming, Dad!* he thought.

Soon they were headed down the river in the direction the silver powerboat had taken.

Mr. St. John frowned ahead at the choppy water. "It's been driving me crazy that we haven't been able to catch Roulain red-handed at his stolen merchandise game . . . and now *this*. Please tell me what's been going on."

Shouting over the wind, George began to explain. He gave the St. Johns the short version of the very long story about how they had found the map and started searching for the diamond and how it had turned serious when Shannon was taken hostage by Roulain.

Mr. and Mrs. St. John were captivated and horrified. Disbelief was evident in their eyes.

George kept going, but it was hard to concentrate. He was worried that they hadn't caught up to Roulain yet. What if they *lost* him? George tried to imagine what would happen after that. They'd have to go to the police . . . but what if Roulain had already done something terrible to his dad?

"Hey, are you sure we can catch them?" he interrupted his own story to ask. He knew he sounded really upset, but he couldn't hide it.

"Oh, we'll catch them, all right," Mr. St. John promised. "You just have to start thinking about how we're going to deal with Roulain when we do. I don't want anyone to get hurt."

Mrs. St. John nodded her agreement and turned back to George. "Now, tell me more about this diamond. You say you finally found it right down in your basement?"

George nodded. "Yeah, it was inside the doorknob of the trapdoor to the tunnels the whole time," he said.

Mr. St. John glanced over from steering the boat. "Well, how did Roulain know about the whole thing? And why was he so keen on getting it that he would kidnap Kira?"

"He's working for the Litarian government, actually," George explained. "My dad says that they're really corrupt and that they probably hired him to get back the Eye of Eternity so they could be more powerful."

"There they are!" Renee shouted. She had the binoculars held up to her eyes. "See them? Right over there."

Roulain's boat was just a speck on the horizon, but Mr. St. John steered toward the speck. They were gaining on Roulain's boat, and George wondered how long it was going to take before Roulain realized they were following him—and about what he would *do* when he realized that.

Nothing but static came from the walkie-talkies.

"I'm going to open up the throttle on the engine, kids, so hold on," Mr. St. John shouted. "Here we go."

Suddenly the front of the boat lifted out of the water and they started *really* moving. George saw Paul's eyes grow wide with wonder as he grabbed Mrs. St. John's hand for reassurance.

After only a couple of minutes they were within a hundred yards of the powerboat. Renee was still watching with the binoculars. "Here he comes!" she shouted over the wind. "He's out on deck, trying to figure out who we are."

"We're pyrates!" Derrick shouted. "And he's in big trouble!"

In a moment they were close enough to see Roulain. He was at the controls, trying to make his boat move faster, but the St. Johns' sleek speedboat had far more horsepower.

"You know, kids," Mr. St. John shouted over the noise of the engine, "I'm not sure about letting you board that boat. Mrs. St. John and I could go, and—"

"Thanks, Mr. St. John," George said, still watching Roulain's boat. "I appreciate that you're willing to do that. But we've been involved in this from the beginning. We're the ones who got my dad into this mess, and we want to help him out of it."

Mr. St. John frowned. "All right," he agreed. "But I'm going with you."

When they got within shouting distance, Roulain just stood out on the deck, screaming at them. He shook his fist, and they could see his face turn red and contort with rage, but they couldn't hear what he was saying over the noise of the engines and the wind.

George looked over and saw Shannon digging through her backpack again. Shannon pulled out a weathered piece of cloth that looked kind of familiar. It was dark and tattered. George realized what it was: the Jolly Roger. She had been carrying the flag around ever since they'd found it in one of the tunnel rooms that was part of one of Captain Kidd's clues.

Shannon shot a smile at George. "I think we might have some use for this now," she said.

"Absolutely," George agreed. "I think we've earned the right to use it!"

Shannon carefully climbed up onto the forward deck of the boat and clipped the flag to the boat's wavering antenna. The other four pyrates watched as the flag whipped defiantly in the nighttime breeze. George felt his throat catch. The time had come: Now they would have to prove that they were a worthy pyrate crew—ready to protect each other, rescue innocents, and make sure that spoils were divided justly.

George looked into the faces of his friends, and their beaming faces told him that they were feeling the same way. They had something to prove.

Fourteen

The Struggle

Carefully Mr. St. John maneuvered their boat so close that they began to be able to make out Roulain's fierce threats.

"You wouldn't dare! I've been searching for this diamond for years!"

Roulain squinted at the approaching boat, and George could see his eyebrows raise as he made out Mr. and Mrs. St. John for the first time. Roulain scowled. *He probably knows he's about to go down for selling stolen goods, too,* George thought. He realized that Roulain had a lot at stake.

"How did you two get involved in this?" Roulain shouted. "This is nothing, I promise you! It's between me and the kids!"

"HA!" Mr. St. John said. He shook his head in amusement and began to maneuver their boat to cut off Roulain's.

"Okay," George shouted to the crew. "We're going to try and board, and once we do, let's just go after him with all we've got and try to pin him down!"

George suspected his dad must be in the cabin, so they'd have to isolate Roulain in order to get inside.

Roulain was still shouting, standing at the controls of his boat. "You'll never get the diamond, kids! *Never!*"

They had passed the Statue of Liberty and were just coming alongside Staten Island. George and his friends would have to jump from the deck of the St. Johns' boat to Roulain's, because there was no time to rope the two boats together. As Mr. St. John got his boat into position for the kids to jump, George looked around. There weren't any other boats on the horizon. Shannon, Renee, Derrick, Paul, and George all lined up along the edge of the speedboat.

"Ready, pyrates?" George asked.

"Ready!" they shouted. One by one all five kids leaped onto the deck of Roulain's boat, grabbing ahold of the railing to pull themselves up. Everyone made it easily—except Paul.

Paul lost his footing for a split second and desperately scrambled to grab a handhold as he dropped off the side of Roulain's boat.

"Paul!" George cried out. His heart was in his throat, but Shannon deftly grabbed Paul's arm, yanking him back up on deck. The only part of him that hit the water at all was his left foot, which left him with one soaking wet shoe.

"Are you okay, Paul?" George called.

"I'm okay, but look out!"

George turned his head in time to see Roulain lunging at him. But George was able to duck away at the last minute, so Roulain didn't knock him down. "I told you kids to stay off! You should have listened! You should have quit long ago!"

George got back up and prepared to dodge Roulain again. Roulain was already running full force. He crashed into George, and they both stumbled to the ground. As soon as Roulain was down, Paul and Shannon descended on him, punching and whacking so that he had to put up his arms to defend himself from the blows. At that moment Mr. St. John jumped over from his speed-boat. Mrs. St. John still stood at the helm, manning the controls. George looked in the window of the cabin and gasped. He could see Kira and his dad tied up inside, with gags in their mouths!

"Dad!" he shouted, completely forgetting about Roulain. Immediately he ran inside. He took the gag out of his dad's mouth first, and his dad immediately started shouting as George worked through the knots in the rope that bound his hands, "George, what are you doing here? Untie me quick! You've got to be careful. He's got a gun!"

George's heart almost stopped. A gun! *I knew*

Roulain had gone bad, George thought, *but I never thought he'd carry a gun—ever!* George leaned out the window to warn the rest of the crew that Roulain had a gun. Roulain was standing up with his back to him.

That was when George realized that Roulain already had his gun out, and it was pointed at Shannon's head!

George watched in horror as he saw his friends' faces go white. He knew he should finish untying his dad and Kira, but he felt like he couldn't move. He couldn't take his eyes off the gun. His friends were lined up with Mr. St. John about six feet away, against the railing to the right of the cabin window.

Roulain was talking quietly but in a furious voice. "You kids are going to regret this, mark my words." He stepped back a few paces but kept the gun pointed right at Shannon's head. "See, George has always seen me as a kind man. But the truth is, I've always had a criminal mind. Back before you kids were even born, I helped run the most successful smuggling and extortion ring this city has ever seen. But then the police caught on to us." He sighed. "I testified against my partner, so the cops reduced my sentence and I was out of prison in a couple of years. I thought, *That's enough crime for me.* I decided to live on the straight and narrow from then on. I got myself a job at Con Edison, and I led a modest little life."

George frowned as he watched Roulain's back through the window. Roulain had a criminal record? Had he really been good, then gone bad again? Roulain seemed completely distracted now. He didn't even seem to realize that as he was holding George's friends hostage, George was still on the loose.

"The thing is," Roulain went on, circling Shannon, "perhaps some people are just born for crime. It's in their blood. Just five years after I'd started work at Con Edison, I was contacted by a Mikhail Zoloc— from a small country called Litaria."

"We know all about Litaria," Derrick interrupted. "We know how you're getting paid by them to find the diamond! How you're helping keep the dictator in place!"

Roulain smiled. "Perhaps. Mikhail Zoloc had a deal for me. If I could find this diamond—which he had reason to believe was hidden in a system of navigable tunnels under Captain Kidd's residence—he would pay me quite a hefty sum of money. And I admit, children, I am not immune to the temptations of fine living. Oh, I was happy enough working for Con Edison and having a humble yet honest life—but presented with a chance to live like I once did? Every whim indulged, every desire fulfilled? I couldn't exactly say no to Mr. Zoloc."

Roulain circled so that his back was facing George. George could no longer read his expression. He glanced quickly back to his dad and Kira, and he could see that his dad had finished untying himself and was rising to untie Kira. He gestured to George to stay quiet.

"So I began searching for this Eye of Eternity. And it proved to be much more difficult than I'd thought. My job with Con Edison made it easy for me to slip into the tunnels undetected—but this is no wimpy rabbit warren of tunnels. This is a huge, dangerous underworld. Years went by, and I was no closer to the diamond. Soon I was running out of time—and money. But I knew that when I found the Eye of Eternity, there would be an enormous payoff. I simply needed money in the interim. So what's a former criminal mastermind to do?"

George couldn't see Roulain's face, but right then he broke into a low, creepy laugh. George shuddered.

"I started dealing in stolen goods. I knew how to handle crime from my former life as a smuggler. The homeless people who lived in the tunnels became a nuisance, so I hired some thugs to keep them in line and, eventually, get them out of there. There was just one problem. I still didn't know where the diamond was. But *then* I learned that you larvae were looking for it, too."

Roulain stepped closer to George's friends, placing the barrel of the gun right up against Shannon's ear. George could see his friend shaking, trying not to look at Roulain. Roulain's voice dropped to a raspy hiss. George could barely hear it over the sound of the water.

"I will *not* be upstaged by a bunch of pesky eleven-year-olds. You think you're so *smart*—finding your clues and following your little maps. But you kids are no match for me. And now you'll pay for being so determined to find that diamond!"

Suddenly, George had an idea: With Roulain's back to the cabin, George was in the perfect position to silently climb through the open window! Carefully, as quietly as he could, he climbed up, pushed his feet and legs through, and gently slid down until his feet touched the deck. He was just a few feet behind Roulain, and he put his finger up to his lips to tell the rest of the crew not to make any signal that he was there.

They all put on poker faces as George crept closer to Roulain's gun hand. With a sharp, sudden movement he raised his foot and kicked Roulain's hand as hard as he could. The gun went flying, finally landing on the deck, where it slid the rest of the length of the boat and dropped into the water with a *sploosh*.

"Way to go, George!" Derrick shouted.

Mr. St. John lunged at the unarmed Roulain, tackling him to the ground. George and his friends jumped on eagerly, forming a huge pig pile.

But Roulain didn't react as if he were defeated. Slyly he freed one arm and reached down to his belt. It all happened so fast, George didn't realize what was happening—*until* Roulain moved his hand away and George saw the huge, gleaming knife in his grip!

Not wasting any time, Roulain let out a chilling laugh and started slashing the air. George's friends jumped up and scurried away from the flashing blade.

But Renee wasn't fast enough. The knife nicked her hand, slicing a nasty cut that began spilling blood onto the deck of the boat.

"That's right," Roulain said in a low voice. "You kids are no match for me. Did you know that I'd been tracking you for weeks, all through the tunnels? I knew when you first found an entrance. And I knew when you found the subway station and the booby traps—"

"What are you talking about?" George cried. "You may have goons down there, but there's no way they know *every* move we've made!"

Roulain chuckled darkly. "Oh, nothing that inelegant for me, George. No, perhaps you remember the birthday gift I gave you. It was very expensive—more expensive than you know, due to all the extras I had put in—"

"The *watch*!" George cried at the same time Roulain said it. He felt so stupid, but how could he have known that Roulain would want to *track* him? "Why would you give me a watch with a tracking device? I didn't even *know* about the tunnels then or the stupid stolen merchandise."

Roulain shrugged. "I knew you were up to something, van Gelder," he said. "You're too smart for your own good. And I know Captain Kidd lived in that house. It was possible that he had left something there—"

"Like a map," Shannon finished. She gulped and looked at Roulain's knife. "Man, you're creepier than I thought. And I thought you were pretty creepy."

Roulain gave her a bone-chilling smile. "Now it's time for you children to disembark, I'm afraid." Roulain slashed his knife through the air and made stabbing motions. "Get ready to walk the plank!" George shuddered—he had never been this afraid. He couldn't recognize his neighbor anywhere in this lunatic.

Paul began to shiver. He turned to Shannon, looking sick. "I don't know how to swim," he whispered.

"Don't worry," she whispered back, "we'll think of something." But the look she gave George told him that she was just as frightened as Paul was. George had learned to swim at one of the city rec centers—but swimming the Hudson River, far away from the shore of Staten Island? None of them were prepared for that.

But just then George caught sight of his dad and Kira appearing from inside the cabin. They must have finished untying themselves! What he saw next made George blink and shake his head. Was he going crazy, or was his dad brandishing a . . . *sword*?

"Where the heck did he get that?" George whispered to Derrick.

"I think it was hanging on the wall," Derrick whispered back. "There were a couple of them over the table in there. But I thought they were just for decoration."

"Not so fast, Roulain," George's dad said in a dark, quiet voice.

Roulain turned around and looked like he couldn't believe what he was seeing. He didn't exactly look frightened. "Oh, please, van Gelder, give me a break. You're going to try to skewer me with an old decorative sword? That thing isn't even sharp."

"Oh, no?" asked George's dad, gripping the sword tighter and edging closer. "We'll see about that, *Leroy*."

Peter van Gelder stepped closer and closer to Roulain, who didn't move. George and his crew stepped aside, careful now to avoid Roulain's knife.

For a moment Mr. van Gelder just glared at Roulain, standing a few feet away, not making a move. Kira stood behind him, tensely watching the scene unfold. Roulain frowned at him like he couldn't believe this was happening. He shook his head slightly at George's dad and rolled his eyes.

"You should try a real weapon, Professor van Gelder," Roulain declared with a flash of his dagger.

Just then Peter van Gelder jumped into action. Lightning fast, he jumped toward Roulain, swinging the sword around in an attempt to land it in Roulain's belly. Stunned, Roulain leaped backward, losing his footing as he skirted the sword. George's dad came at Roulain again with the sword, cutting his pants leg. Roulain's face turned purple. *"You'll pay for this, van Gelder!"* he screamed. He lunged at Mr. van Gelder with the knife.

But it was the wrong move. George's dad stepped deftly aside, leaving Roulain off balance again.

George couldn't believe this was happening. He rarely saw his dad do anything athletic—other than carrying a stack of books. Since when was he an expert fencer? What else was his dad not telling him about?

With one deft thrust of his sword, George's dad knocked Roulain's knife into the water. Roulain tried hard to regain his position, but Peter van Gelder was too quick. He backed Roulain up to the very edge of the deck until the blade was flush against the skin of his throat.

"Very smart, van Gelder. You want me to jump over-
board with the diamond in my pocket? Either I drown
and you never see it again, or I swim to shore and you
never see it again. And I'm a *very* strong swimmer."

Everyone looked over the railing into the
Hudson River. The current was churning, and the
wind was making little whitecaps on the water. It
did *not* look swimmable.

Mr. van Gelder laughed. "If you were that strong
a swimmer, you'd have already jumped in."

Roulain glared at George's dad and eyed the
water nervously. He seemed to be considering his
options. Swimming the Hudson River would take
tons of skill, and surely Roulain knew that.

George couldn't help feeling *really* impressed
with his dad. He could not believe how well he
was handling this situation. He was glad his
friends were all there to see it.

"Roulain, put your hands up. You know you're
not really going to jump into that icy water."

Roulain looked slowly from George's dad to
George and his friends. His face was bright red
with anger and humiliation. George knew that it
must be killing him to lose to a history professor
and a bunch of kids. But he had no choice.

Everyone looked on without saying a word.

"Okay, now let's tie him up," Mr. van Gelder

said finally. He was busy holding the sword at Roulain's throat, and Mr. St. John was standing guard off to the side, so George and his friends would have to handle the rope. Kira found some rope in the cabin and handed it to Derrick.

"Don't come near me, you little brats! You're not *touching* me," Roulain shouted.

"Watch your mouth, Roulain," George's dad said, poking him in the neck with the sword. "Or you can jump in and see how deep it is."

George and Derrick came forward and tied him up, Roulain grumbling and protesting the whole time. Once the knots were secure and both Mr. St. John and Renee had approved them, a silence seemed to fall over the boat. No one knew what to say.

At last Peter van Gelder spoke up. "Kira," he said, glancing back at her, "why don't you go into Roulain's shirt pocket—very carefully—and take out the diamond so we can have a look at it."

Kira's face brightened. "The Eye of Eternity! I can't believe it's been found at last!" She walked over to Roulain, smiling at George and his friends. "Your father told me about the adventures you children have had. I can't thank you enough for your bravery. To see such a precious jewel!"

"Get away from me, you Litarian fool!" Roulain hissed. "Your monarchy will never see this diamond!"

"Actually, before I do that, perhaps I should take care of something," Kira suggested. She went back to the cabin, then came out again with a roll of duct tape. "I spotted this in the cabin," she said. "It's good for many different things. You never know when you might need it."

She unrolled a long piece, ripped it off, and carefully placed it over Roulain's mouth. "Now maybe you'll refrain from saying hurtful things."

"UMRGHGRGB! RUUUNHDGH!" Roulain cried as she reached into his shirt pocket and took out the Eye of Eternity.

"Wow. It is even more beautiful than I could have imagined," she told Roulain cheerfully.

"RRRRGHMMBBBB!" he replied, red-faced.

Kira didn't pay any attention to him. She placed her hand on Mr. van Gelder's arm. "I'm so relieved you're all right, Peter. We're so fortunate that these kids showed up when they did. Thank you so much, all of you!"

George felt himself smiling. Her appreciation was so sincere, it was hard to believe that just yesterday, he had been convinced Kira was up to no good. "We're just glad you're okay, Kira," George said. And he meant it.

"Ahoy!" shouted Mrs. St. John, who had watched the whole event from her own deck. "Well done, van

Gelders and friends! Toss me that rope on deck and we'll lash these boats together."

Peter threw her a rope, and together he and the St. Johns got to work connecting the boats.

As soon as she was able, Mrs. St. John jumped on board.

"I knew you were up to no good, Roulain! I don't know why you thought you could get away with it," she told him with a frown. Then she turned to George and his friends. "What a brave bunch you all are!" she said with a big smile. "Now, let's have a look at that diamond I've heard so much about."

Renee held the diamond out in her good hand, and Mrs. St. John oohed and aahed.

"I went ahead and called the Coast Guard when the skirmish started on deck," Mrs. St. John said. "They should be here in a few minutes."

"Oh. Well, I'm glad to hear that, Eleanor," Peter van Gelder said.

"What did you tell them?" George asked.

"I said we were in the act of apprehending a kidnapper and international jewel thief and could they please send someone to arrest him."

Peter nodded and gave a little smile. "That sounds about right."

While they waited for the Coast Guard to arrive, Mrs. St. John tended to Renee's cut and then they all made themselves comfortable on the deck of Roulain's boat. To the west lay the subdued lights of New Jersey, and to the east was the beautiful New York skyline.

George reflected on the last few hours. On the one hand, he felt happy—they'd found the diamond, caught Roulain, and gotten Kira back safely. But on the other hand, he felt sad seeing how very bad his friend had become. He had really liked Mr. Roulain. He had been a cool and understanding guy who always treated George with respect.

But that Roulain was gone. George didn't know which one was the true Roulain anymore.

Fifteen

SHARING THE SPOILS

"It's so heavy," Shannon said, holding the Eye of Eternity for the first time. "And I can't believe how sparkly it is, even in the dark."

"Yeah," Derrick agreed. "It really is spectacular. I can't wait to get my share of the money and get that new bike I've been wanting. That, and I'm going to buy my mom a brand-new computer for her business. She's going to be so psyched." He took a swig of his soda and leaned back with a satisfied grin.

"Wait a minute, Derrick," George said. "We never really decided whether we were going to keep the diamond. I mean, it's not really ours."

"What do you mean, George? We found it. Why wouldn't we keep it?" Derrick asked. A little worry line popped up between his eyebrows.

"Well," George said, knowing that Derrick wasn't going to like what he was about to say, "it was stolen to begin with. It *really* belongs to the Litarian people."

"Sure, it belonged to them like three hundred

years ago. None of the people it belonged to then are still alive today, right? And we risked our *lives* for it," Derrick protested. "If it wasn't for us, that diamond would have sat in that doorknob for another three hundred years. Shouldn't we get some sort of reward for that?"

George sighed. "I don't know, Derrick. The Eye of Eternity belongs in the scepter. It means a lot to the people of Litaria," he said. "And I really believe from everything I read in the journal that Captain Kidd wanted the diamond to be returned to its rightful owners. He set up this treasure hunt in the hopes that the diamond would be found by someone honorable enough to give the diamond back. He didn't mean to steal the diamond and was never able to give it back to the Litarians during his lifetime. But he knew that it was rightfully theirs."

"Wait," said Shannon. "With all that Kidd has put us through, don't you think he owes *us* a little something? I mean, why go through everything we went through if we're just supposed to give the diamond back in the end?"

"I dunno. I can't explain it, Shannon," George said. "It just feels like the right thing to do. But it's not up to just me. What do you guys think?" he asked Renee and Paul.

"I think it should go back to Litaria and be put

back into the scepter," Renee said. "No question. It could really help them."

Paul looked at his four friends' faces. "I don't understand," he said simply. "The diamond was theirs, and somebody stole it? Then we should give it back. I don't need a diamond."

Derrick looked incredulous. "You mean to tell me that you guys don't want the money?"

"Of course I want the money," Renee said, "but how can you enjoy something if you've really taken it away from somebody else?"

Shannon looked at Derrick and sighed. "She's right, you know," she said reluctantly. "Much as I would like that money after all we've been through . . . it doesn't belong to us. It never really did."

Derrick frowned. "Well, when you put it that way, I guess I see what you mean," he said, still looking disappointed. "All right, then, I give up. We should give it back."

"I'm very proud to hear you kids say that," Peter van Gelder's voice said from behind them. George looked up and saw his dad standing over him. He hadn't even heard him sneaking up. "If you want to give it back to the Litarian people," his dad went on, "the best person to give it to would be Kira. She's on the board of the museum where the scepter is kept, and she would see to it that the scepter is put back in the right hands—with the diamond in it."

"Yes, that's true," Kira agreed. "It's my fondest wish that the Eye be returned to its place in the scepter and that the scepter remain the property of the people, as a symbol of their brave history."

"Well, then, let's do it," George said. "I guess we should just hand it over. No time like the present."

Everyone agreed enthusiastically.

George took the diamond from Derrick and walked over to Kira, followed by his four friends. He stood in front of Kira, and his friends made a circle around the two of them. Carefully, willing his hands not to shake, George held out the diamond and cleared his throat.

"Kira Trenov, on behalf of the entire pyrate crew, I would like to transfer ownership of this diamond, the Eye of Eternity, from us to you. Please return it to its rightful owners, the people of the country of Litaria, with our best wishes of hope for their future."

Kira had tears in her eyes as she took the diamond out of his hand. "You can't imagine what this is going to mean to my people," she said quietly. "I never thought I'd see this day. On behalf of the Litarian people, thank you. I'd also like you to know that I think the deposed monarchy is going to be extremely grateful. This will give them the chance to regain power, and I expect they will want to honor you in some way."

Out of the corner of his eye George could see his dad smiling. "What do you think they'll do?" George asked.

"The king might invite your group to their residence-in-exile in Austria and confer knighthood on each of you," she said.

"Are you *kidding*?" George cried. "We get to be *knights*? That's amazing!"

"Whoa," Shannon agreed, "that's almost as good as being pyrates!"

"Definitely," Renee said with a huge smile.

"You can't put knighthood in the bank," Derrick grumbled, but when they looked at him, he was smiling, too. "Oh, come on, you know I'm kidding," he said.

"What's a knight?" asked Paul, looking pleased but confused.

"It's like a special friend and protector of the king," Shannon explained. "A huge honor. It's very cool."

"Cool," Paul agreed with a laugh. George looked on with a happy feeling.

Just then the lights of the Coast Guard boats came into view from up- and downriver. "Looks like your time as a free man is up, Roulain," Mrs. St. John said.

The next hour or so was a flurry of activity. The Coast Guard boarded the boat, took Roulain into custody, and then went around the boat taking statements from everybody.

"Do you have any hard evidence?" one of the officers asked.

"Actually," Derrick said, pulling the handheld computer out of his pocket, "this might help you a lot. It belonged to Roulain, and we used it to figure out where this boat was kept. It has lots of names and addresses and schedules—people who bought from Roulain, people who stole for Roulain."

The officer took the computer and smiled. "Sounds good." He turned to George's dad. "These must be some pretty brave kids," he said.

"Absolutely," Peter van Gelder agreed, with a smile.

George couldn't remember the last time he'd felt this close to his dad.

It was pitch-dark when the authorities finally finished up. Everybody boarded the St. Johns' speedboat to head home.

"Let's get home and take it easy," Mrs. St. John said as her husband started the engine and turned the boat around. "I'd say this was a *very* full day."

George felt himself getting sleepy as they drifted back to Manhattan. He sat with his friends on a bench near the back, and they were all quiet, watching the lights of the city draw closer.

"Paul," Mrs. St. John said warmly, "how would you like to try steering the boat?"

Even from several feet away George could see Paul's eyes light up. Paul looked at Shannon, who nodded, and the two of them stepped over to the steering wheel in the middle of the deck.

"Here's how you do it," Mrs. St. John began to explain, and Paul listened carefully before trying it himself. He didn't say much at first, but after a while Mr. and Mrs. St. John had him talking about everything from their adventures down in the tunnels to how much he loved Oreos.

When Mrs. St. John started to ask about details of Paul's life, he hesitated at first. George could tell that Paul was nervous to talk about where he slept and how he found food, but he slowly started to answer those questions, too.

"Paul," Mrs. St. John said eventually, and George could hear a funny tone in her voice, maybe a nervousness. "How would you like to stay with me and Mr. St. John for awhile, in our house?"

Paul was silent for a moment. George couldn't see his face in the darkness, so he didn't know what his expression held.

"We live right next to George," she explained.

"Ummm," Paul said finally. "I don't know. Is there

a bed there, like the one I saw in George's room?"

"Yes, there is," Mrs. St. John said eagerly.

"Are there Oreos?" Paul asked. "George's house didn't have Oreos."

"Well, we could stop on the way home and get you some, if you like," Mrs. St. John said, laughing. "If you like Oreos, wait till you try my chocolate cake."

"Hmmm," Paul said. "I guess that would be okay. For a little while, maybe."

"So, yes?" Mrs. St. John said. She sounded excited. "You'll stay around awhile? George will be next door. And you can call Shannon on the phone whenever you like," she told him.

"I'll give you my cell-phone number, Paul. Then you can reach me anywhere," Shannon said, putting her arm around him.

"Okay," Paul said, smiling shyly.

At the marina, George's dad put Shannon, Derrick, and Renee into a taxi, giving the driver plenty of money to get them home. Everyone called, "Good night!" and, "See you tomorrow!"

"Hey," Derrick said to George right before he got into his cab, "I meant it when I said you came up with some brilliant stuff today, George. Really. We're all really lucky that you're our captain."

George felt his face flush with pride. "Thanks, Derrick."

"Anytime." Derrick ducked into his cab and shut the door. "Later!"

"Have a good night, van Gelders," Mrs. St. John called from the sidewalk before getting into another taxi. The St. Johns and Paul were heading to the deli to get some Oreos.

"You too, Eleanor," George's dad called. "We'll see you soon."

"Bye, Paul," George called, waving after his new friend. Paul glanced back and smiled. "Bye, George," he called. George heard him ask Mrs. St. John, "What's a *deli*?"

George and his dad laughed and turned to face Kira, who was smiling shyly.

"Well," she said softly, "I suppose I'll head back to my apartment. George, I can't thank you enough for what you and your friends have done."

George could feel himself blushing a little. "Anytime," he replied. "I guess . . ." He looked up at his dad and smiled. "I guess we'll see you soon."

"Right," Kira replied warmly. "I'll see you both soon. Good night, van Gelders!"

"Good night, Kira!" George's dad called as Kira turned and headed to the subway. Together, he and George began to head home on foot.

"You know, my friends all thought you were pretty cool tonight, Dad," George said. "And so did

I. I had no idea you knew all those fencing moves. That was amazing!"

Peter van Gelder chuckled. "Thanks, son. You pulled some pretty fancy stunts yourself. I wish your mother were here to be part of this. She'd have loved figuring out the maps. You definitely got that talent from her. She probably wouldn't like the fact that you broke two promises to me in one day, though," he said with a short laugh, "but we'll let that go, just this once."

George looked up at his dad and nodded. He felt tears sting his eyes, but they weren't just tears of sadness from missing his mom. They were tears of pride, too—pride in himself and in his dad.

"It'll be nice to get home, won't it?" Peter van Gelder asked, putting his arm around George's shoulders. "We can make some hot chocolate and relax. Maybe we can even pull out one of your mother's old jazz records."

George smiled. He could still remember the melody of one of her favorite songs. It would be good to hear it again. "Sounds good, Dad," he replied. In a few minutes they were walking through their front door.

The kitchen was still pretty messed up from Paul's search for Oreos. The maps were still all laid out on the table, just as they had left them when they went downstairs to retrieve the Eye.

"I'll start cleaning up the kitchen. How about you put these maps somewhere safe?" George's dad suggested. "They're historical documents and family heirlooms. We may even look into donating them to a museum."

George nodded. He couldn't really imagine parting with these maps now, but leave it to his dad to think of the historical significance.

"I'll put them in your study for now, Dad," he said as he carefully piled them up. "Is that okay?"

"Sure." George's dad had already busied himself straightening the counters and closing drawers. George clutched the four maps to his chest and then carefully slid the wooden chest that had held map three into his arms.

"Be right back!" George took the stairs carefully, not wanting to drop anything and ruin the memories of their great adventure. He looked down at the carefully drawn maps, and he couldn't help feeling a special connection with Captain Kidd— the man who had led George to his treasure. At various points while they looked for the diamond, George had begun to wonder whether Captain Kidd really had good intentions. Some of the booby traps were pretty nasty, and some of the things they'd found along the way—corpses, weapons— had made him wonder what Captain Kidd was really up to. But the way Kidd had laid out this whole adventure, making sure that whoever found the diamond would be worthy enough to give it back to Litaria, impressed George. He felt pretty convinced now that Kidd had been a good guy.

George was so lost in thought, his foot missed the last stair, and he was suddenly thrown off balance. "Uh-oh!" he cried as he struggled to stay up, but he could feel himself tumbling toward the landing. "Oh, no!" George clutched the maps to his body, hoping they wouldn't be damaged, but the chest slipped from his grasp and clunked down to the floor. George winced as he made contact with the landing. It hurt, but at least the maps were safe.

"George! Are you okay?" George's dad called from downstairs.

"I'm fine, Dad," George called back, but he could hear his dad running up the steps. George looked around—the maps were fine, but the chest had fallen on its side and the lid had been knocked open. And actually . . .

George blinked. The chest had been empty when they'd taken out the map, but it looked like a bunch of yellowed *papers* had fallen out.

"George?" Peter van Gelder appeared behind George on the landing, and George struggled to get to his feet. "Are you sure you're all right?"

"I'm okay, Dad," George insisted. "But look at this! There was something else in Captain Kidd's chest!"

George stood up and walked over to where the chest had landed. Carefully he picked up the handful of papers and then lifted the chest to look inside. George's dad peered over his shoulder. A new flap of wood hung loose, hinged to the bottom of the chest. George lifted it and saw a small compartment at the very bottom.

"A false bottom!" George's dad whispered behind him. "Ingenious and tricky—just what I'd expect from Captain Kidd! What are the papers?"

George glanced quickly at the familiar, scripty writing that he now recognized as Captain Kidd's.

Received worde that an emissary from Litarian Republic . . .

George abruptly stopped reading. "They're pages from Captain Kidd's journal," he explained. "Captain Kidd must have ripped them out and hidden them for some reason."

George's dad frowned in puzzlement. "Hmmm. What do they *say*?"

"I can't be sure, Dad," George said, heading for the phone. "But I think this calls for an emergency pyrate meeting!"

Sixteen

Kidd's Secret

"Hey, Renee, pass me a slice of pepperoni?" Shannon said, handing her plate across the table.

She had to shout to be heard above the din of laughing and talking. It was an hour after George had found the hidden papers, and all of the pyrates, along with Kira and the St. Johns, had rushed over to the van Gelder house for an emergency meeting. Paul and the St. Johns had just arrived, and everyone was still munching on a newly delivered pizza and goofing around. They were all still in high spirits from their amazing victory that evening.

George threw out an imitation of Roulain as he was getting tied up. *You pesky kids! I'm going to get you! Just as soon as I get out of prison!*

As usual, George's imitation was dead-on. Derrick laughed so hard that he knocked his drink onto the linoleum floor. He grabbed the mop from the utility closet and started using it to parry like he had a sword, going after George.

"Take that, Roulain! And *that,* you kidnapping smuggler! I'm Captain Peter van Gelder! And I'm going to be on the Olympic fencing team!"

Kira laughed hysterically at this, so hard that she spit out her soda and had to put it down. George thought it was pretty funny. He was beginning to think she was actually kind of nice.

"All right," Shannon said as soon as she could talk over the laughter. "We're all here now, George. What's so important?"

"Yeah," Derrick added as he sat down on one of the kitchen chairs. "What's up? The diamond's found, Roulain is with the police. What else is there for us to worry about?"

"Well, I don't think we have to *worry,*" George said with a smile. "You're right, everything's worked out now. But when I was putting the maps and everything away, I dropped Captain Kidd's wooden chest—and these fell out." George held up the papers. Everyone strained to see, and then they oohed and aahed.

"They look like journal pages," Renee called out. "Is that true?"

"Yeah," George said. "I think Captain Kidd ripped them out and hid them in a secret compartment in his little chest. And I have a feeling, since they were locked up, that they must say something important."

"Well, let's see," Shannon said impatiently.

George laid them out gently on the table, and everyone gathered around.

"Wow, it's really hard to read," Mrs. St. John said. "You told me all about the maps, but this is the first I'm seeing of these artifacts up close. To think that they're three hundred years old!"

"If you don't start reading, *we're* going to be three hundred years old," Shannon said. "Come on, I'm dying to know what it says."

"Okay, here I go," George said.

They all looked down at the papers. The writing was in fancy longhand script, obviously written with a quill pen, with strange letters and funny spelling. They were pretty hard to read.

"Be patient, okay?" George said, and began:

14 June 1699

Received worde that an emissary from Litarian Republic is in transit to Newe York for the purpose of retreeving a large diamonde of which I am in possessyon. The diamonde belongs to the Republic and was stolen from their Royale Scepter during the last war. Called by them the "Eye of Eternity," it came to me on a recent mission and shall be returned to its righteful place in order to abide by my second oathe: "Never steale from those who do not deserve it." The Litarians will have their diamonde back.

"I can't believe it!" George's father said. "He's talking about Kira's ancestor, Sergei Trenov. That's who was sent to retrieve the diamond!"

George felt a prickle up the back of his neck. He glanced at Kira for a minute, wondering what she thought of all this. Kira had told him that she thought Captain Kidd killed Trenov, which had really made George angry at the time. But then they'd found Sergei's grave down in the tunnels. It was true that Captain Kidd had probably killed him, but George believed that Sergei Trenov might have tried to double-cross him and that Kidd had killed him out of self-defense.

Kira returned his gaze, wide-eyed. "Perhaps now we will learn the truth," she said gently.

"Let's keep reading," he said, and continued slowly reading aloud:

23 June 1699

Expecting Sergei Trenov, emissary from Litaria, to arrive on the morrow, on the ship "Fidelity" from London. He will lodge withe Sarah and myeself.

Looking forward to meeting withe him and returning the diamonde. It is a quite beautiful jewell.

"So he *wanted* to give it back," Shannon said. "And he didn't want to kill Trenov, obviously. Something must have happened. Keep reading," she told George.

"Okay," he said, trying to steady his voice. He glanced at Kira, and she nodded. She looked a little confused, but curious. They were finally going to find out what had happened to Sergei Trenov and how Kidd had ended up with the diamond.

24 June 1699

I have passed an enormously enjoyable eve withe the emissary from Litaria, learneing of the fascinating historey of a stronge and noble people. Trenov was moved and thrilled to tears to be able to hold the Eye of Eternity in his hands. It is a sacred object for his people and consydered divine. Trenov is an engaging man, and Sarah and I stayed up long into the night discussing matters of politics and religion withe him.

"So they really liked him," George said softly.

"That appears to have been the case," Kira agreed.

"I always believed Kidd killed Sergei to keep the diamond. I always thought he was the villain! Now I'm not sure what to say."

"Well, let's finish Kidd's story." George went on:

30 June 1699

A terrible mystery has fallen upon our household, and we are scarcely eateing or sleeping for the pain of it. Our houseguest, Sergei Trenov, emissary from Litaria and excellent newe friend to us, has disappeared. He stepped oute from our house early morn three days ago to take a morning constitutional walk, and he never returned. Foul play is almost a certainty, as he left with only his topcoat and hat for warmth and left behind not only his belongings, but also the sacred Eye of Eternity, which of course was the reason for his trip from the continent. We are lost.

George had to stop for a minute because the page he was reading was so brittle, it felt like it was going to crumble. He gently smoothed the page and held the edges down carefully with his hands.

"George, keep reading before I have a heart attack!" Shannon said.

"Imagine. They went through all this right here in this very house!" Mrs. St. John said.

"But what? Went through what? What happened?" Derrick said. "Come on, George."

George continued reading:

25 May 1701

My heart is heavy and sits like a stone in my chest. I am hiding like a prisoner in my own home, writing by candlelight in the darkness of my own basement in the middle of the day. How can the sun shine outside when inside me it is black as night? The newspapers of several days ago spoke of the capture and hanging of me, Captain Kidd, King's Privateer. They said that I had been captured by soldiers of the Royal Army as I was leaving my home in Newe York and returned by ship to London, where I had been hanged for the criminal that I am. Yet here I sit, alive and breathing. I am certain the man who has been killed is none other than my friend Sergei Trenov, mistaken for me as he left my home. I knew the throne was turning on me, but I never expected to be hanged. How could I have known in order to warn my friend? How can I go on knowing I have caused this fine man's death? What shall I do? My wife, Sarah, is my only consolation.

"Holy moley! That wasn't Kidd who was hanged in England. That was Sergei Trenov! This is unbelievable!"

George burst out. "This explains why they say Kidd insisted that he was innocent, that he wasn't even himself as he was being hanged. It really *wasn't* him!"

"Oh, my. I can't believe this!" Kira said, leaning against George's father.

"What else does it say, George?" Peter van Gelder said, putting his arm around Kira. "What happened next?"

George took a sip of soda and read on:

As I live and breathe, I will dedicate the rest of my days on this earth—given to me as an unwitting gift by Sergei Trenov—to making sure the Eye of Eternity is returned to its rightful place in the Royale Scepter of Litaria. I am creating a hideing system that will be impenetrable to all but the sharpest minds. I am hard at work digging and setting traps, and soon I will emerge from my long hideing period. I will assume a new identity and change my appearance and live out the rest of my life quietly, trying to do good work and harm no one. My days of adventure are over.

I will be known from now on as the gentleman "Ulysses Pyle." I will wear a beard and long hair, and I will court the beautiful widow of Captain Kidd, one Sarah Oort. I hope to marrye her soon. If you are readeing these pages from my journal, you may be close to finding the treasure. Please abide by one of my most closely held oathes: "Share all spoils justly." To those who come after me: The Eye of Eternity belongs to the people of Litaria, and it is my life's wish that it should be returned to its righteful place.

The group sat in stunned silence. It was George's father who finally spoke. "If Captain Kidd was actually Ulysses Pyle, then that means you *are* really related to him, George! You are a true descendent of Kidd!"

"That's right! Sarah Oort was your great-times-eight grandmother, so Kidd must have been your great-times-eight grand*father*!" Derrick practically shouted.

George could hardly believe it. This was the best ending he could have thought of to the most amazing adventure of his life. Or if he was actually the descendant of a real pirate—maybe his life's adventure was just beginning.